## BOOKS BY ADAM KLEIN

*The Medicine Burns*
*Tiny Ladies*
*Jerome: After the Pageant*

✳ ✳ ✳ ✳ ✳ ✳ ✳ ✳ ✳ ✳ ✳ ✳ ✳

# THE GIFTS OF THE STATE

## NEW AFGHAN WRITING

✳ ✳ ✳ ✳ ✳ ✳ ✳ ✳ ✳ ✳ ✳ ✳ ✳

Edited by **Adam Klein**

**db**
DZANC
BOOKS

**DIS|QUIET**

**db**
DZANC
BOOKS

# DIS|QUIET

5220 Dexter Ann Arbor Rd.
Ann Arbor, MI 48103
www.dzancbooks.org
www.disquietinternational.org

This book is a work of fiction. Names, characters, places, and incidents are either products of the authors's imaginations or are used fictitiously. Any resemblance to actual events or locales or persons, living or dead, is entirely coincidental.

Jawad, Abdul Shakoor, "The Hasher" first appeared in *Witness* XXVI.2 ("Redemption"), 2013.
Atif, Khalid Ahmad, "The Sea Floor" first appeared in *Guernica Magazine*, August 15, 2013

Cover art: Yanik Wagner.
Photo: Hoshang Sulaimanzada—the inspiration for "The Grape Tree."
Book design: Steven Seighman

ISBN: 978-1-938604-55-3
First edition: November 2013

The publication of this book is made possible with support from the National Endowment for the Arts, and the Michigan Council for Arts and Cultural Affairs.

Printed in the United States of America

10   9   8   7   6   5   4   3   2   1

*This book is dedicated to the memory of my mother*

# CONTENTS

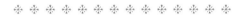

# ACKNOWLEDGMENTS

Many thanks to Dzanc Books, the writers anthologized herein who gave so much of their time to this project, Chin-Sun Lee, who listened closely as I read these stories to her over the years, my colleagues at AUAF who supported me in this work. *Witness, Guernica Magazine,* and *The Saint Petersburg Review* for publishing stories, in slightly different form, from this anthology, and to *Fourteen Hills* for providing me space to talk about this book.

# FOREWORD

*My fingers said to my pen,*
*soon we'll be dust but you'll remain.*
—Afghan folk couplet

The stories collected in *The Gifts of the State* include some of the most essential written by young Afghans today. Emerging from their teacher Adam Klein's writing workshop in Kabul, they represent the challenges of growing up in Afghanistan right now.

The tales in this collection range in genre. There's *The Hasher's* deceptively simple parable of the traditional rite of swara, in which a young girl is given in marriage to fulfill a blood debt between two families. *The Pleasure of Judgment*, written by a young man rather masterfully in a woman's voice, is a sci-fi thriller about the devil's arrival in Kabul via Blackhawk helicopter and the seventy-two lesbian Huris of Paradise. There are three terrific stories by women: *The Second Sister*, *The Snow over the Stones*, and *Ice Cream*. In *Hardboiled*, the tough-talking Mickey Spillane inspires the soft-core imagination of an undercover bookseller during the Taliban regime. And most unforgettably, there's *The Sea Floor*, a haunting story that straddles three worlds as it struggles to make sense of the inexplicable violence and horror that is part of the nation's current burden.

The brutality of unspeakable massacres, sex, war, cultural contradictions, the legacy of Russian occupation, the hypocrisy of the Taliban, the uneasy relationship with U.S. Forces, the country's looming future—these stories examine at close range some of the irreducible images and experiences of life for Afghans under thirty.

Yet it's far more than subject matter that makes these stories worth reading. The clean prose and fully wrought perspectives, which I suspect reveal Adam Klein's patient work with each of these writers, render the quality of these Afghan stories in English a rare feat. Too often, we miss the best of Afghan writers, whether in Dari or Pashto, because good translators are nearly impossible to find, and many of the finest writers don't speak English. The authors'—and Klein's—dedication to this emerging literature appears on every page, in the vivid prose, the elegant storytelling, the arresting characters.

Not once does a reader sense that these stories have wandered from their sources or are forced into translation because they aren't. For this collection, Klein worked with the writers in English from the start. For many, as he points out in his introduction, English is not a second, but a third language. This is one of many reasons why these writings are so undeniably present to us.

—Eliza Griswold, New York, February 28, 2013

# INTRODUCTION: AFGHANS AUTHORING AN UNCERTAIN FUTURE

## ADAM KLEIN

✽ ✽ ✽ ✽ ✽ ✽ ✽ ✽ ✽ ✽ ✽ ✽ ✽ ✽

For over two and a half years the stories came in from creative writing workshops I offered in Kabul. It was, for many of the young writers collected here, the first time that they were asked to compose a story: their own or someone else's, someone they'd only heard about, a lost relative, someone born before their time—the choice was theirs. And so the project *The Gifts of the State: New Afghan Writing* emerged. The stories stuck with me, sometimes quiet, pastoral narratives detailing how villagers cooperate and sacrifice together, and sometimes how villages unravel under the burden of tradition. There were, of course, stories of ethnic violence, a city carved with checkpoints, militia affiliations, and boundaries that are crossed out of love and hunger. The stories frequently show little affect in the telling. The Taliban and mujahedeen are more prominent in this collection, more problematic than Americans or Russians, their legacies more contested.

History, even fictionalized, written primarily by former refugees, is inevitably contradictory, colored by countries of origin, places where writers spent most of their formative years. The writers collected here sit side by side in direct conflict. Some write of the martyrdom of the mujahedeen; others, of their petty brutality. They write of marginalization suffered in Pakistan and Iran, and despite this, they also write of falling in love in exile, relationships broken off by their return to Kabul once the Taliban fled. Stories of disappearances under the Russians, of Afghan communists now quiet about their former lives, and of successful battles that ultimately routed the Russians are all equally weighted.

Surprisingly, a number of male students attempted to write from a female point of view. I once imagined that physical gender segregation would also create a prohibition between one gender adopting the voice of another. Not so. Women wrote freely in the voices of men, of the indifferent abuses committed by them, and also of the quiet animus between women who'd stayed during the Taliban period, and those who'd returned years later in "western clothes," seemingly exhibiting those foreign values.

We began workshops with examples of short fictions, mostly online, from around the world, including E.C. Osondu's *Waiting*, V.V. Ganeshenanthan's *Hippocrates*, excerpts of Svetlana Alexievich's *Voices from Chernobyl* and *Zinky Boys*, *Vast Hell* by Guillermo Martinez, and many others. We talked of voice, physical description, organization, the mechanics of story writing. But I did not encourage them to write only of sad things, tragedies. I didn't offer much in the way of prompts. I did say that Americans, and probably most of the world, rarely read of how Afghans love, how they negotiate a culture respectful of their elders and avoid perpetuating the same ethnic conflicts their parents may have enacted. The writing was simple, mostly chronological, without pyrotechnics, but unsentimental and visceral. They asked for permission to write about things they felt taboo, often after they'd written them.

Imagination, I suspect, is a bit like a muscle. *Start off easy,* I advised my students, *with those situations you feel confident conveying.* This isn't every teacher's approach or even necessarily the right one; it was merely what I asked of them. I hadn't begun with a book in mind, though that soon followed. I became invested in their willingness to share their experiences, or the way they were told about, or remembered, the past. They had no fear of fictionalizing, were happy to author, or at least radically revise, the past. These authors write of personal conscience silenced by cultural or religious norms, of freedoms that Americans cannot provide, or that some Afghans are not prepared to take. At the heart of these stories is the difficult knot of religion and culture, as though this was easy for anyone to untangle. Afghans often take pride in conservatism; for decades it has drawn "true believers" from around the world—the best and worst of them. Imagine, then, those authors who question the crueler beliefs, ones not in the Qu'ran but practiced as though they were religious edicts.

In America, and broadly in the West, when an injustice occurs, we ascribe it to an individual's own volition; the media draws psychological portraits of such people as drifters, lone wolves, those who have crossed the line between fantasy and reality, frequently without anyone knowing they've done so. This is why Shirley Jackson's story *The Lottery* was taught to us in elementary school; the idea of communal, systemic violence is an American prohibition. When confronted with the abuses of Abu Ghraib, our administration and our legal institutions insisted on "bad apples," and quickly dismissed our cultural acceptance of anti-Muslim rhetoric and intolerance as "unfortunate."

In Afghanistan, suicide bombers, the abuse of women, of drugs—these issues are not easily perceived as performed by people who've fallen through the cracks, or people with mental health problems. Even "mental health problems" is new vocabulary. Communal guilt cuts both ways; it enables societies with weak civil law to keep crime low (everyone is responsible for everyone), but it also hampers open discourse of such things as extremism, sexism, child or spousal abuse. Rather than the violence of a few marginal zealots, it is believed to reveal something at a culture's bedrock. In other words, Afghans haven't yet found the separation between the country's fringe and its tolerant majority, so it's harder to configure what is or should be acceptable, what is a personal failure or a cultural one. And then, of course, Afghanistan's conservatism has drawn scholars, but more often jihadists, who imagine the country's enemies easy to identify. I think of the young John Walker Lindh and his Arab and Chechen compatriots making their trek to Afghanistan, pursuing what they imagined were abuses *against* the Taliban. If morality—the "right" war, the right belief—was only that easy, we would never have seen an Afghanistan ground to rubble or talk of the Bamiyan Buddha "shells." Collective shame over extremism is one reason to encourage individual voices of conscience. This, I felt, was the promise of a collection of young Afghan authors. I imagined my job was to gather from a few aspiring writers the larger possibility for voices in a country too easily collectivized by frontline reports, historians who make Afghans seem like undefeatable warriors incapable of love, humor, heresy, let alone creating peaceful homes or democratic assembly. Too often we disregard the individual experiences of Afghans for the historical narrative. I can think of no other country where this is so tragically engaged.

For my workshop participants, English is often at least a third language, not spoken in the home. Reading in English is rarely done for pleasure. These writers don't live in the rhythms and cadences of American authors, can only name a handful of them, and don't understand tone enough for the easy use of irony or sarcasm. Most don't feel the need to break with form or enter the speculative. What *can* be said, and the effect of telling, is still being tested in this post civil-war society. For this collection I chose stories close to completion that had a distinct, if quiet, voice; at least a nascent story I hadn't heard before; and took risks. I then worked one-on-one with these writers to fix grammar, offer suggestions for tougher verbs, suggest the addition of some physical detail, provide some ideas of how a scene might be better integrated—what any editor might do to make an author's work read more smoothly. Inevitably, one can attempt to be hands-off, but this was an overall framework and ideal. I was careful to step out of the way, to avoid making the work more "literary" than it already is in its mostly plainspoken way. To the best of my ability I guided these writers while letting the stories remain theirs. English offered a chance to speak of what they dared not discuss in Dari or Pashto, to an audience "out there"—one they did not need imagine, at least for a while. Sometimes I had a couple of meetings with a writer; others required a couple of months of one-on-one editing. We worked through the stories to go deeper, to exploit techniques available to them. They wrote of the anxious present moment, just barely able to trust that the past is the past and not the prelude. "That's why it's time to write it now," I enthused. Though, once the stories took shape, these writers rarely required any outside influence to complete them.

Afghanistan in its present form is as new to many Afghans as it is to Americans. The mass exodus of so much of its population during the wars makes it hard for Afghans to ascribe blame for the dissolution of their society, or to imagine how to rebuild it. In vogue now (in Kabul at least) is blame for the I.S.I. (the Pakistan intelligence service), the "backward" provinces, or Pakistan itself. None—or at least very few—of these writers mention Unocal's pipeline deal with the Taliban, the neo-conservative impact on the militarization of the region, the Islamic revolution in Iran, the policies of Afghan president Hamid Karzai, or the Americans, despite the news reports in which a few thousand Afghans burn effigies and shout "death to America." Destabilization by either Pakistan or the American departure can return Afghanistan to the fundamentalism that failed them before. Afghans know they will not be left alone, that there are still proxy wars to be fought, regional advantages, and mineral wealth to exploit. Now, with Afghanistan again foisted onto the geopolitical stage, these writers wonder how soon before the interest from the outside world will wane, and just what outside interest means in the shaping of their country.

I remember a few years ago sitting in writing workshops at The New School, and the confidence and (sometimes) competitiveness of its participants, everyone imagining their lives being of interest to others, worthy of representation and publishing advances. Do "reading cultures" ultimately result in a kind of narcissism? Afghanistan certainly shows no sign of a niche fiction market. Twenty-somethings who have faced death, walked across mountains to live in refugee camps, would likely not make a great adventure story for a country measuring out what to forget and what must not be forgotten. Americans exploit and frame and sell these stories; Afghans merely live them, and put them behind them. Even images from the 1970s surprise my students, that Afghanistan had a history of rock bands and artists and tourists rather than NGO workers and gonzo journalists. They forget Afghan women worked in maxi skirts. It's unthinkable now. The amnesiac power of "purifying" regimes—this is what authors can stand against.

As in many countries, a family name is the book you're born into in Afghanistan, the essence of historical meaning. By "meaning," I refer to influence, not of countries, but of families who are sometimes as ruthless. Otherwise, you are born into the working masses, still mostly agrarian, with their unbending traditions. In a culture like this, what is the point of an individual's travails? How can a story be seen as one's own, or engender respect? And yet, in writing these stories, I think these authors began to believe in their power to transform, if not their society, then the "outside world." Why else ask if I could assure them that the book would not appear in Afghanistan? Would anyone who graduated with me in New York want their writing to be available anywhere in the world *except* in the United States?

My friends in the U.S. speak of "occupation," about allowing Afghans to determine their own futures. I hope this introduction will at least suggest that a coherent, pre-existing Afghanistan was mostly destroyed by the wars and a subsequent amnesia that drifted in waves through its streets like the smoke of ordinance. No one here shares the same view of who his or her liberators or oppressors are or were. Neither Russians nor Americans seem particularly reviled (again, Kabul is likely quite different than Kandahar in this sentiment). Some of the students' parents were communists, and today it's not surprising to find cab drivers speaking Russian, unimaginably talking of the beauty of Siberia—a place I'd grown up only hearing of as a penal colony. The students have exile minds—by which I mean that they can't conceive of a world where destiny won't encroach: they insist the Taliban will never again gain a foothold here, but are afraid to return to their own provinces where the Taliban have infected many with a unifying dream of simple and immediate justice, under which so many suffered.

Ultimately, I learn from them: one writer tells me of the confusion he experienced when he accidentally dropped his mother's hand at a busy bus stand. It was his first time seeing her outside the home and in a *chador*, the unique, face-covering burkha worn in Afghanistan. In that moment, he saw that every woman looked identical, every mother could be a stand-in for his own. Later in life, when he dawdled after school to play a game of soccer and saw one of those blue sentinels from the corner of his eyes, she became an *everymother*, a totem of conscience. Is it any wonder the sexes might mix differently there? And then there are those men who stayed during the Taliban period, describing the feeling of nakedness as they cut their beards with dull scissors after the Taliban fled their villages—men who looked grizzled before their time, suddenly boyish again, covering their naked cheeks with their hands.

These writers straddle a new world of global banking and NGOs, dressed in business suits one day, and wearing traditional Afghan attire the next. They don't consider it a jump between past and present. They don't see themselves as the authors of either. Life, whether they write about it or not, is already written. Outside their windows, a surveillance balloon circles the mountains in search of men with rocket launchers on their backs. The science fiction of daily life is naturalized here, just as the Taliban's "stone-age" justice was just an adaptation, an erasure of problematic "secular" values. And now, they are asked to consider their own experiences, or their own imaginations, but for which readership? I, for one, wanted to see how they'd use the tools of fiction, whether they could give voice to those singular people the news has too often made featureless, collateral.

Tomorrow is impossible to predict, I remind them. We don't know where we'll be, where the country will be. Stories keep silence and amnesia from rising like dust and obliterating life as we know it now. *This is a dusty country*, they remind me, but still they return for each individual appointment. The writers carefully suggest, "This, I think, is the stronger word." And dutifully we replace it.

# THE GIFTS OF THE STATE

✳ ✳ ✳ ✳ ✳ ✳ ✳ ✳ ✳ ✳ ✳ ✳ ✳

# THE HASHER

## ABDUL SHAKOOR JAWAD

❊ ❊ ❊ ❊ ❊ ❊ ❊ ❊ ❊ ❊ ❊ ❊ ❊

The village Nahrebala had nothing but harmonious people and a big stream that flowed in the middle of its fertile lands. The padawan would take the cows, sheep, horses and donkeys from the villagers and graze them in the rich pastures beneath the western mountains. The weather was cold and the mountains full of trees used for winter fuel. The wild river, after hitting hundreds of large rocks, would flow from the middle of the mountains all the way to the eastern borders of the village, and even further to the next province. Trees encircled each house, and the village itself was separated from other villages by denser forests. Houses were made of clay and wood for the most part. The distance from the new city was far enough to make the villagers arrange their visits only on a weekly basis, and those who needed to go went together. The rest of the week, they would spend their time working in their fields. It was the only source of income.

In order to help each other, the villagers had something called *hasher*, volunteer work in the field of any villager who called for it. Everyone in the village had the right to call hasher. The host would then provide good food for the workers at lunch. This was not only an event of zealous work but also of great socialization. Jokes, bluffing, sometimes wrestling, making fun of each other, discussions about the climate and, of course, working, were the main activities of such collective labor. The women would stay at home, take care of the children, and prepare food.

The winter was nearly ending and people of our village were planning on cultivating their wheat. Our family was the first to call for hasher. I went to search for all the tools we had in order to facilitate the harvest. I found some of the tools we needed: shovels, axes and the like, but there were too few to accommodate the number of people who would work our land, so I went and borrowed the rest from our neighbors. I gathered them in the corner of our yard beside the room where we kept our animals. The night passed. My father and I went out early in the morning to make sure everything we needed was present before the villagers arrived. We worked on leveling the field until the first man showed up.

"Look! He never comes second," my father said, pointing to Qazi Mama arriving with his shovel on his shoulders. By the time Qazi Mama reached the field and greeted us, other workers began to leave their homes and make their way over. Qazi came with his two sons Ajmal and Faisal. Mahboob, Qazi's younger brother came with his fifteen-year-old son Karim. My cousins, Jawad and Saifullah, also arrived. The only other person who was expected to come was Hayatullah, who was Qazi and Mahboob's elder brother, but he did not show up. The workers picked up their tools and followed my father's instructions.

"The soil is very hard," said Qazi, hitting a clod with his naked foot. "But not harder than you," said my father. "Oh! There he comes, Mr. Chief Guest," said Mahboob shouting to Hayatullah, who was coming very slowly towards the field with his six-year-old son, Bahram. "You should have taken a lantern with you," my father said, and the other workers laughed.

Hayatullah would always carry his Russian Kalashnikov with a leather belt. He put his gun in the corner of the field beside a tree. Hayatullah took a shovel and started working on the soil. The work got serious. The sun felt like a set of hands on our backs. There were three hours of work and after that the workers demanded a tea break, and I was the one to bring it. I went home where my mother prepared tea for the guests and I returned to the field, balancing the tray of small glasses. The workers sat dispersed and began chatting with each other and drinking.

Everyone started in with each other and Hayatullah was the focus of our kidding because of his style of speaking, the way he would look angrily at Qazi, and most importantly, how he would swear on his white hat by taking it off and hitting it on the ground. The funniest part was when he would pretend that a djinn had taken hold of him, and he would begin beating himself, as though to rid himself of the others' recriminations. Today, the joking was not as bad because of everyone's exhaustion from the heat.

Only Qazi Mama would not give up. "Was it you who used to steal hens?" he asked. Hayatullah continued looking down as if he heard nothing, but when everyone started shouting at him, he threw his shovel aside, came toward Qazi, and told him that he was the biggest liar in the village, saliva from his mouth hitting Qazi's face.

"Why then do you always hide from the old women of the village?" asked Qazi, wiping his face with his sleeve.

"Because you are not a Muslim, you annoy the weak and fear the strong, after all, you are my younger brother and you should respect me," said Hayatullah.

✳ ✳ ✳

The tea break was over; everyone went back to their places and continued leveling the land until it was lunch. I called upon everyone to wash their hands and gather beneath a tree where we would normally collect the harvest. It had good shade and there was a folded gray carpet spread out. I cleaned it of leaves. My younger brother Tariq came and told me that my mother was calling me. I knew that the food was prepared. I started walking towards home and on the way I saw Bahram holding his father's Kalashnikov. He was taking it from its belt, then, raising it to his chest, aimed at something. "Be careful boy," I told him.

I went directly to the kitchen, which was located in the middle of our house. A thick layer of smoke covered the wooden ceiling beams; they were completely black with soot. The kitchen was all clay work and it had an uneven stairwell of clay, too. I climbed the stairs to see if the food was ready to be served but I ran back to the door when I heard a gunshot. I knew that it was Bahram. From the door, I saw all the workers gathering around one person lying on the ground. I ran and ran until I reached the crowd where Hayatullah was lying insensible, blood flowing from his chest. He was hit with five bullets. He was severely injured and no one thought that he would survive. Bahram was also crying next to his father. Soon after, people from the village were rushing towards the field and I did not know how to react to the situation for it was the first time I'd heard of death, and the first time I'd seen it.

Qazi was the first to realize that Hayatullah was no longer alive. He bent down and closed his eyes, then took his handkerchief from his waistcoat and wrapped Hayatullah's head with it.

"Go and get a woven bed from your house," Qazi said hastily. I rushed to the house and took the bed and came back to the field without noticing how I got there and how I returned. We put the deceased on the woven bed and raised it on our shoulders and the whole crowd was following us all the way to Hayatullah's house. Bibi Gula was standing in front of her house when we brought her dead son. She was screaming so loudly and with such anguish that almost everyone was in tears. My father took care of Bahram so that no one would harm him.

The relatives of Hayatullah were coming one after the other until his house was full of people. The mullah of our mosque came, too. He started inquiring about the murder.

"The deceased should not be kept at home any longer. We should bury him as soon as possible," he advised. The funeral started immediately. Qazi and Mahboob washed Hayatullah's body. Mullah Haya Khan led the funeral prayer outside the mosque. The deceased was then taken to the graveyard. The grave was dug one meter deep, two meters long and sixty centimeters wide. We put Hayatullah in that grave and put some flat stones on top of him, not touching him. Then, everyone was hurrying to cover the stones with soil. The shovels were there and people participated, taking their turns burying him. When the dirt rose to a mound, the mullah preached to the crowd and reminded them of the inevitability of death. The funeral was over. Everyone went back home. I too went home with my father.

In the morning, I heard that Mahboob, the brother of Hayatullah, was intending to kill his nephew to avenge his brother. Lyla, the widow of Hayatullah, was from a neighboring village. I told my father about Mahboob's intentions and he told me that Hayatullah was wealthy among the villagers and Mahboob wanted to deprive Hayatullah's son and heir so that his wealth would go to his brothers. It was not until lunch that my father and I were invited to a jirga in the house of Mohammad Jan.

"Please, my son is innocent. He is only six. It was unintentional," said Lyla beating the door of Mohammad Jan's house where the elders of the village were gathered to decide the fate of Bahram. I thought so many times to go out of the room and console her, but I was a witness who needed to be there in order for the just elders to determine whether or not to kill Bahram. Mohammad Jan hosted every jirga in our village. He not only had wealth and power but also had a very sharp mind and had recently solved a major dispute between two families of our village and that of the neighboring one. The other attendees of the jirga were Mahboob, Qazi, Aminullah, the brothers of the deceased, and Subhan, the maternal uncle of Bahram. My father and I were witnesses.

The brothers of the deceased insisted on killing their nephew for the general rule in the village was an eye for an eye, irrespective of age. Mahboob, the elder brother of the deceased, was sitting next to Mohammad Jan reclining on a pillow shaped like a ship.

"There is nothing to be said or told about the general rule of our village. We will kill the boy and we have the right to do so," said Mahboob, leaning forth and beating the carpet with the back of his hand. Qazi and Aminullah praised their brother and said that this rule was an old rule and must be maintained. No one in the room disagreed with the rule. Subhan declared, loud and clear, that he would avenge his nephew no matter who killed him or what jirga justified it. Hearing this, Mahboob's eyes grew bigger, his forehead forming four waves. We could see he wanted to jump on Subhan and finish him but he did not utter a single word.

After a pause, Mohammad Jan got up and sat in front of Mahboob and put his hands on his lap and told him that killing Bahram would not do him good for Mohammad Jan foresaw a new enmity forming. "Fear Allah, and suppress this satan of yours who demands nothing but taking the life of an innocent soul."

"We will lose our dignity by not killing the killer of our brother," said Mahbood, his voice rising.

"The village has always respected the one who forgives his enemy," said Subhan. By now, the only change I observed was in the faces of Qazi and Aminullah.

"We have only one way to resolve this and that is that Sub-han's daughter is going to be married to Mahboob," said Qazi, and Aminullah nodded. Mohammad Jan went back to his place and Mahboob looked down as if he were reflecting. Subhan said that his daughter was only twelve and Mahboob was forty.

"If you want your nephew forgiven, then this is the only way," said Mohammad Jan turning his face to Subhan.

The jirga was adjourned and Subhan requested some days to think about this. After a week, we heard that Subhan agreed to give his child to Mahboob. The wedding party was arranged for the next week. The week had passed and both families were preparing for the wedding that in no way was like a union people usually celebrated.

None of our family members attended the wedding party and from that day forward, there was no more hasher in our village.

# THAT COWARD, NASEER!

## ABDUL SHAKOOR JAWAD

✳ ✳ ✳ ✳ ✳ ✳ ✳ ✳ ✳ ✳ ✳ ✳ ✳ ✳

On a hot summer day in 1990, I was playing with a dog in the yard. My mother came and told me, "Why don't you go and sit with your father and his guests in the guesthouse. You may learn something from them."

"What will I learn?" I asked.

"Your father is the head of the Department of Education of the Islamic Party of Afghanistan. This is why he always has guests and meetings and they never come to a decision."

"What decision?"

"Oh son, do I have to explain all this right now? There are seven parties and they're always fighting about who's going to get the money. Don't ask too many questions. Just go to the guesthouse."

I said "OK." On the way to the guesthouse, I saw my uncle, our only relative in Peshawar, holding an image of someone I did not know. I asked him who the person in the photograph was.

He replied, "The party leader."

I was excited. I wished to have a closer look at the image and when I touched the mounted photo in my uncle's hands, it fell from his grasp to the ground. I was slapped for my disrespect. I lowered my gaze out of shame and meekness and followed the path to the guesthouse where I was supposed to learn from the elders. I entered the room and saw some ten people sitting and reclining on fat, red pillows.

My father called to me, "Did you say 'Salaam' when you first entered?"

I said, "Yes."

"Then go and shake hands with everyone." I shook hands with every guest and I repeated my name ten times. Each guest asked me my name, as though none could hear the other, or me. An elaborate ceremony was under way. Then, my father told one of his friends sitting beside him that I knew the fundamental creed of Islam. They all said that they wanted to hear it so I started reciting in the middle of the room, my face sweating and my gaze lowered. They all applauded my recitation. My father sat me on his lap and started chatting.

Mansoor, who had a black turban on his head, told my father that I was a smart child and that my father should enroll me in school earlier than other boys of my age. He argued that if I learned Arabic, I would be a leader in my future, with access to Arab money. My father refused and said that I was too young for school. Then, one of the guests started talking about other party members. He was very angry and cursing those members who were perceived to be corrupt. The other guests agreed. I did not know what was going on but I took pleasure from the company of the elders who had applauded me.

The Soviet Union was frequently mentioned. Some of the guests would say that many children were killed by the Soviet Union. Others would say that the occupiers had faced their due and just fate. I did not know if the Soviet Union was a country or a person. It seemed to me a defeated, merciless monster. The stories about the Soviet Union increased until I feared it, imagined it killing children and feasting on them. I asked my father why the Soviet Union was doing such things. He replied with such hard laughter that I was not able to grasp his answer, if he had one.

My uncle came in and brought tea for the guests. Everyone, including my father, stopped talking. I heard a whisper that my uncle was a member of another party. My uncle went to the back of the room and began to hang the photograph he had slapped me for knocking out of his hands earlier. He hung it beside a photograph with another serious man's face on it.

The guests started talking about the militia groups again. One of them said that the Islamic Party would have the greatest share in the communist defeat in Afghanistan.

"We, too, have lost men. We will fight until the last," said my uncle proudly. A tension came into the room, and the other guests and my father looked down for a while. After my uncle left, my father said, "This is the only problem I worry we all will face. One of you, take down both pictures."

Mansoor said, "The future leadership of Afghanistan belongs to the Islamic Party."

"I know this. We all know this," my father said. "I don't want any tension in my house. Take down both pictures."

As someone rose to remove the photographs, I heard the sound of my cousin Naseer and took the opportunity to go outside to see him. We started playing and I took a stick and told him, "This is my gun and I will join the militia groups when I get stronger."

He replied that he did not like fighting, and walked off.

# THE GIFTS OF THE STATE

## SOROSH HAYATI

Late afternoon, when I opened my eyes, I looked through the window of our small room; everywhere a fog crept, thick as fur. I had slept all afternoon, and another dull day passed. The snow enabled me to imagine the city very calm, quiet, sleeping profoundly beneath its cover. I wanted the sun never to rise; it would melt the snow and expose the rottenness and memorials in the vicinity.

I woke up by myself. What had happened that my mother hadn't woken me, shouting, "Bahmeen, Bahm, get up; it's late. You have slept all day, you'll die sleeping."

I called, "Mom, what do we have for din...."

My voice slowed then stopped. The word *mom* rang in my ears. I repeated it to myself, *mom, mother, mom*. A sentence recurred, one that my mother often repeated: "Mummy and you are one." I felt helpless as I repeated this, and I felt a sorrow so vast it could not be contained. I couldn't tolerate listening to anything that reminded me of the word *mother*.

In the calmness of the room I heard the crash of a ladle in the pot and dishes in the kitchen that had been both our dining room and bedroom, and the buzzing of an old folkloric song my mother used to hum, sewing needles in her mouth. Sometimes she inserted my name inside the verses of poems, "You my love, you my life, you my soul, you my Bahmeen." Those sounds rustled in my ears like hidden spirits, like the wind in trees. The room was still. I couldn't tolerate staying in that house; my mother was trying to talk through its simple implements and the old songs.

On a big hook on the wall next to the door of my room, a dark green coat was hung with symbols that showed the accomplishments of its owner, and there was a pair of boots, one boot stuffed in the right and another in the left pocket. The jacket belonged to my father, who was killed by militias twenty-one years ago in this district, before I was born.

I remembered as a child that my mother had tried to put me to sleep and would tell me about my father's pride, honor, and self-sacrifice. That's how he had saved this district. He wasn't militarily trained but was nonetheless a patriotic man. When renegade fighters planned an attack, they marched into the southern part of our village. Over time, they began regular incursions, committing robbery and violent crimes against the civilians. My father, with a group of his friends including Mohammed Maher, Hakeem, and Harar, who are all now living in an apartment in the city, planned to force them out. All I know is a roadside bomb killed my father. The government gave our family the military uniform, a medal and some cash.

My mother had pointed her finger, saying, "Look at your father's shabby shoes; they are tattered from running and fighting in the mountains." While telling his story, her eyes teared up.

She said to me, "If I live long enough, I want to see you in that uniform. I want to see you in those new boots."

I put the coat on, laced up the boots, and walked to the door. My footsteps fell on the wooden floor. My feet felt numb; someone else's feet who'd been walking a long time. I stopped and looked back, then headed for the kitchen. Again the reminders of my mother moved in the atmosphere, turned it like something in an old pot. I left the house and the door ajar, even though I imagined that the winter chill would lace the inside of the windows with ice.

I kept my hands in my pockets, and snot ran from my nose. My head hurt because of the frigid weather. I tightened my fists in the pockets of my father's jacket. My body was shivering, not so much because of the cold, but because I was going to meet my mother.

I was thinking how joyfully she would react if she saw me in this outfit. I kept walking downhill until I neared the village, Hesar, where my father was buried. Every week my mother went to visit the grave but she complained that the town was too crowded. They could not be alone together any longer. Long ago I had stopped escorting her, sensing that I had no place between them.

As I made my way into the city, onlookers were passing, wrapped in their shawls. Some looked confused by my uniform. Others seemed to be hurrying before night fell. I could see the surrounding streets, a few lamps and the lights turning on in the store windows. There was a candy shop in an alleyway that I remembered visiting with my mother. I thought I would buy *sheerpera*, a kind of sweet, made with milk and pistachios, which she always loved. When I left the shop, people were passing in horse-drawn carriages and old cars. A middle-aged lady slowed down, opened the window and called out to me. "Hey, hey hello. Where are you going?"

At that moment, I became confused. Without considering it, I said I was on my way to see Mohammed Maher, Hakeem, and Harar. I told her I thought they lived in the center of town in one of the new buildings.

"Get in, I can take you there. Nobody has come to visit them in so many years. They'll be so happy to see that you've come back." I sat in the front seat and looked at her. She was familiar to me, but I wasn't sure how. In fact, I asked if she were Hakeem's wife, without ever having met Hakeem.

She said, "No, but I had once loved him, just as I had loved all the men who fought for this village." She was very formal and kind, as if she were really talking to a military officer.

I was astonished at how I replied. I looked at her eyes and after a few minutes asked, "Do you know my mother? I brought these candies for her, but now I think I should take them to my father's friends."

She said, "They have been waiting for you. Your mother used to bring them sheerpera. Sometimes she made it herself."

She turned her face and looked warmly at me, and then quietly drove the rest of the way. The city was full of people walking with vegetables under their arms, waiting for the bus, shaking each other's hands and kissing each other in greeting. But there was something *not* happening. The embraces went on too long, and it seemed as though people were standing at the bus stops— not impatiently—but as though they never expected the bus to arrive. One man, closing his shop, appeared to be rolling down the gate an infinite number of times, as though a short video loop of him were playing over and over. Even the woman driving me appeared to be traveling the same streets; the same thin, dark buildings reappearing.

The woman stopped the car in exactly the same place she had picked me up. "This is where they're all living now," she said. "You'll need to take the stairs. The elevator hasn't worked in twenty-one years."

I got out of the car and entered the metal door of a Russian-style apartment building, badly damaged by rocket fire. I made my way up the stairs but my father's boots were so heavy, it seemed time elongated as I reached each floor. Eventually, I arrived at what might have been the top of the building, though I have no idea where it was. A door was open and my mother stood, holding it wide. "At last you've come, Bahmeen. I hope you brought the sweets for your father and his friends."

Inside the room, my father looked as he did in photographs my mother had once shown me, but he was animated, slapping the couch and inviting me to sit beside him. Hakeem, seemingly much older, was smoking and singing the folk tune my mother used to sing, "You my love, you my life, you my soul, you my Bahmeen." My mother laughed, pulling me by the arm into the room where the four fighters were reunited and celebrating an eternal victory, spending their small government allowances in their perfectly new uniforms. When I offered them the sheer-pera, Harar shouted, "The Candyman, Wakil! Still makes the best sweets in town!"

We sat laughing and enjoying ourselves. I sat with my mother and father on either side of me, and their friends talking, remembering. Later their wives joined us. Some of the women put up tea, and we heard the pot whistling in the other room, but no one hurried to take it off the flame. It seemed we could happily stay there forever. Whistling, too, was the wind from the vast hole in the wall where a rocket had smashed its way through twenty-one years earlier. It whistled like a rotten tooth. It seemed like we had been drinking tea and eating candy our whole lives.

# MULES

## BAQIBULLAH NIAZI

✳ ✳ ✳ ✳ ✳ ✳ ✳ ✳ ✳ ✳ ✳ ✳ ✳

I was shocked to see aunty Rahellah. She was almost unrecogniz-able. She stood at the checkpoint holding a bag covered with dust and a can of cooking oil. Aunty Rahellah was one of those miserable widows who kept trying to deliver food items from Chahar Asiab district to Kabul for more than two years. Trans-porting these items was considered smuggling by Hezb-e-Islami. I, too, would be called a mule.

Aunty Rahellah's family and mine were neighbors for more than five years when her husband was alive, and we still met each other almost every time we went to deliver goods to Kabul. As I came closer to her, I saw sorrow in her face. Normally a strong lady, now her expression showed weariness. I approached her, wondering what tragedy had struck that had changed her to this extent in only two months.

She was facing another woman almost her same age and was saying, "This world is not for people like us. Not for us to enjoy. We can't have a simple life but must be pushed, beaten, killed." I looked at her and thought, this is not aunty Rahellah. Only her voice is the same.

She asked, "Qasim, is that you?"

I replied, "Yes Aunty! How are you and where is Fahim?"

"I'm OK son," she said, and turned back to the woman she was talking to and dismissed her with her hand.

"I don't see Fahim," I continued. "Is he with you today?"

"Didn't you hear about him?" she asked.

"No Aunty, what happened?"

Fahim was just two years younger than me, aged fourteen. He was slight, with thin shoulders, a long, serious face, and a sharp mind.

He would ask, "Will a day come when my mom stays at home with my sisters and I can bring them food and everything they need?" My response was always "yes" but I wasn't sure. It wasn't a time to be sure of anything.

Aunty Rahellah choked as she explained. "Three weeks ago, when we brought some rice, oil, and flour to our family, one of the mujahedeen at the checkpoint shot him in the leg."

She was sobbing, so I asked her to sit. We both went close to a cracked mud wall that seemed it could collapse at any moment. We sat in its dusty shadow. I was struggling to start the conversation about her son again, to hear his name on her lips.

"Sorry Aunty. For Fahim," I said. After a deep silence I asked her, "Why did they shoot a fourteen-year-old boy and nobody else?"

She started with a stutter. "He was the only man in my family. How could they? When we arrived at the checkpoint I saw a huge, terrified crowd of people shouting, crying, talking without listening to each other. I asked Fahim to return to Chahar Asiab and go back the next day, but he refused."

She looked at me and said "Qasim! I wish he had listened to me but he didn't; his two younger sisters were hungry." She started crying again. She said, "He warned me if we stayed here overnight, they would die of starvation."

I was still in my seventh class of secondary school when the communist regime fell and the mujahedeen entered Kabul in intimidating, marauding gangs. It was a sunny afternoon when someone knocked on our front door and called me to come out.

I yelled to him while running toward the door, "I'm coming. I am coming, wait a minute."

When I opened the door, I asked, "Are you crazy? Why were you knocking on the door like you're being attacked by a dog?"

It was Fahim. We both went to a road just two blocks south of my house in Khair Khana and welcomed the groups of armed men by joining them in calling, "God is great, God is great." They were seated inside the back of their Toyota trucks in huge numbers, driving slowly, welcoming people one by one.

I turned to Fahim and pointed to the appearances of the men. "Look at their long hair, Fahim. Did you see the one carrying bullets around his vest and on his shoulders? What is he going to do with that many bullets?"

Fahim replied, "Probably fight another invader." We both laughed and walked toward our houses before darkness fell.

Soon after the mujahedeen's arrival in Kabul the situation turned bad. All the government offices were looted and everyone who had worked within the government was left jobless. My father and Fahim's father were both sacked. The war for power had begun and the city was divided into many regions. Days and nights passed with only a slight difference: the struggle for power became a struggle for survival. The southern and southeastern corridors to Kabul were closed off for food items by Hezb-e-Islami. The scarcity of goods made living in the city impossible. My two younger brothers and I started delivering rice, flour, fuel, and cooking oil in small quantities from Chahar Asiab district at the same time aunty Rahellah and Fahim also began their illicit smuggling. It seemed entirely natural to meet them at the Hezb-e-Islami militia checkpoint about twenty kilometers to the southeast of Kabul; there were no other options. We would have to face the militia's fidgety troops each time we traveled back and forth into the city.

Aunty Rahellah was well known among our neighbors for her beauty, but her son's murder shortly after her husband's death took away her hope—the real foundation of that beauty—forever. Her face now appeared lined and dark, too full of shadows. She was bent like she had lived with sorrow and hardship for more than a hundred years. After several minutes of talking I was still looking for my answer.

"Why was he shot?" I again asked her. "Aunty! How did it happen?"

"He went to talk to Rauf to get consent to cross the checkpoint but Rauf had found out that he was trying to fool them, pretending his leg was injured. He ordered his fellow colleague to shoot Fahim instead of giving him permission."

We had been squatting by the mud wall, and my legs began to cramp. I held my aunt's arm and helped her to stand, her bag and cooking oil sunk in the dirt. I heard a bus rattling in the distance and picked up aunty Rahellah's belongings.

"Let's take that bus that's coming," I said.

"There is no way you can cross the checkpoint in the bus," she said.

"I have an idea Aunty, let's go."

The bus arrived in a cloud of dust. I turned around and punched my nose several times in order to get it to bleed. Aunty Rahellah yelled at me, "Are you crazy? Why are you doing that?"

I then pushed aunty Rahellah toward the bus doors and ordered her to get on. We sat beside each other in the back, my nose still running and my hands bloody.

She whispered to me, "I can't see you with a broken nose. Please stop doing this."

I knew that the people at the checkpoints were too selfish to look at someone who needed medical assistance. Instead they would ignore their presence. If I hadn't broken my nose to cross the checkpoint, we would have been pulled out and jailed in a hot, dirty shipping container.

The rusted bus squealed every time it hit a bump, and in a few minutes we reached Rauf's checkpoint. We were stopped and one of the militia with a long beard and dusty hair got on, searching people's luggage for food items and fuel. He passed both of us, pretending that our seat was empty. The bus started up again and we drove a couple of minutes toward the city. The hills outside the windows looked so arid one could imagine water didn't exist on the planet. Their outposts were built of rocks and bags of sand. Their roofs were just rough cotton tied to four posts, and they flapped noisily, sending up clouds of dust each time they did. We entered a very narrow valley called Sangeh Naweshta just five kilometers to the north of Chahar Asiab. Only the main road and a dry river crossed the valley at this point.

Aunty Rahellah said, "Fahim was trying to do what you just did but he didn't make it."

I told aunty Rahellah "God will punish them. He will give you the strength to support your family."

After sighing deeply she replied, "Yes son, he will." But the burden of Fahim's death still sat between us. We both grabbed our bags when the bus stopped. I said goodbye to her, but it was the last time I saw her. I don't think she believed there were any more tricks to be played. I don't think she ever tried to cross a checkpoint again.

# THE VILLAGE RADIO

## ISMAIL HUSSAINI

✤ ✤ ✤ ✤ ✤ ✤ ✤ ✤ ✤ ✤ ✤ ✤ ✤

Akbar was the only literate man in the village of Bala Deh. He was a graduate in mechanical engineering from Saint Petersburg. He entertained the villagers with stories of Russia and his time there. Bala Deh is only a hundred miles west of Kabul. Akbar came with his old brown Russian radio to the mosque to inform the elders that last night there was an attack on America. Uncle Rahim was the eldest and looked worried upon hearing it.

"Now, we are in big trouble," he said quietly.

I walked with my father and my younger brother Ahmadshah across the lawn of the mosque. We walked for about half an hour but said nothing to each other. Each of us was lost in thoughts we did not share. My uncle, Mr. Quraishi, and his only son, Fahim, came late to the mosque and found everyone worried.

Mr. Quraishi, with his coarse sense of humor, walked toward Akbar and asked him if his loving wife had passed away.

Akbar shouted, "Mr. Quraishi! That is really not funny. We are discussing an issue of significant importance for the future of our village and our children."

Fahim looked embarrassed by his father's silly joke and was angry at the same time. Fahim had been married a few months earlier with the youngest daughter of uncle Rahim, and didn't want his father's recklessness to create problems with his in-laws. Uncle Rahim came forward and told all those villagers to gather again in the fields in front of his house after the afternoon prayer.

Men moved toward uncle Rahim's after prayers and some children were already in his front yard. Other children were playing in the fields nearby and a few of them were eating apples from the trees. A big tree, believed to be a hundred years old, cast finger-like, accusatory shadows at the surrounding fields.

Uncle Rahim sat under that huge tree and removed a dried stamen from one of its flowers with his shaking hand. Then all the villagers sat in a circle and waited for the elders' advice. Uncle Rahim's grandson Mahmood brought two big kettles and some glasses. Ahmadshah moved forward to help Mahmood serving green tea and some Kabul sweets.

Mr. Quraishi stood up and asked, "Why are we here today? Can someone please tell us the reason? Don't you know that if the Taliban is informed that we have gathered here, we will be killed?"

Uncle Rahim said, "Mr. Quraishi, we know the risks and that is why I have told everyone to gather at my house, not in the village mosque. You are not as wise as your son, Fahim."

Mr. Quraishi grew angry and shouted. "Yes, Fahim my son is a wise man because he is the slave of his wife, and you are happy because he obeys your daughter."

Akbar came forward, "I think you should stop discussing your family problems here. We are here to discuss issues of interest to all the villagers. Maybe we can solve your personal problems later."

Uncle Rahim stood up and threw the material of his long turban over his shoulder. It was white and crisp as his long beard. He explained that Akbar had said last night there was an attack on the U.S.A. and two tall buildings were hit. "This attack on the U.S. government has caused great anger among Americans because many individuals were killed and injured."

I went to Akbar and asked him, "Who attacked them and what else did the news on the BBC say?"

He shook his head like he knew nothing more than that. My father said, "I know it is none other than the Russians. Russians have always been the biggest enemies of the Americans."

Akbar said, "As far as I know, and what I understood from the news, it seems like some Muslim extremists are responsible. And I think that the Taliban, with the support of Saudi Arabia, has arranged this attack."

Ahmadshah with his straggly brown beard asked, "How will the attack on the Americans affect us? We are thousands of miles away from them. The elders of the village have always told us that America has never been interested in Afghanistan. There is no reason that today we should care about them."

My father angrily pointed at Ahmadshah and told him to keep quiet. Uncle Rahim continued. "If a fight between the Taliban and the Americans begins, innocent people will die. To gain financial support, the Taliban will loot everything from the people. That is the reason we have asked everyone to get together today to discuss our future plans. But before taking any action let's listen to the news on Akbar's radio," Uncle Rahim suggested.

Akbar proudly returned with his relic and sat near uncle Rahim and all the villagers settled down near the old tree. Akbar managed to tune in the BBC in Farsi on his radio and we heard the reports. Fahim, Ahmadshah and a few other villagers who were sitting behind the others jumped from the crowd as if they were seeing something live. Uncle Rahim's grandsons and a few other children climbed on the branches of the tree to listen to the scenes described on the radio. We all understood that hijackers had hit two towers and thousands of people had died. But there was no clear idea of who had arranged and supported this terrible attack.

After listening to the news, discussions among the villagers continued for long hours with no specific outcome. One of the grandsons of uncle Rahim came running; he announced that the Taliban pickup trucks were coming toward us. In seconds, everyone disappeared from the scene. I helped my father to hide under some bushels of wheat that the farmers had recently collected. A few minutes later we came out from under the bushes and looked for Ahmadshah but could not find him. I looked at my father's eyes and could see he was weeping. I asked him what had happened.

"When I was in the army many years ago making the rounds from village to village, all the villagers stood up in rows to see us. They used to bring milk and hot bread to feed us. But today everyone hides. People called us communists but weren't afraid of us. I'm not sure we were communists; we just supported the Russians. I don't even know whether these Taliban are Muslims. Why would we fear them if they were?"

I smiled at him and said, "Dad! You were communists."

Slowly we moved towards our home, bending back the reddish yellow wheat of our farm to get there. Winds from the south were moving it like small choppy waves. Birds sang beautiful songs but my father was worried, concerned the birds would eat all the wheat by evening. We entered our house and seeing Ahmadshah there at home made us happy. He was standing before the dresser, removing a photograph of our mother. "Let's make sure we hide this in case they come," he said, sliding it under the cloth that protected our Qu'ran.

It was a one-floor mud house with three bedrooms, a kitchen in the yard and two big stables for our livestock. My mother came with a glass of black tea in her shaking hands. She asked, "Is everything OK in the village? Why were you all at Uncle Rahim's house today?"

My father said, "It is a long story. I will tell you late tonight. Prepare the bathroom; I want to take a shower."

The next morning after prayers Mullah Jamil, a man in his early forties, dressed in black clothes and carrying a Russian Kalashnikov on his shoulder, came with an alert from the Taliban government. He proudly announced the coming of another holy war. They wanted men aged above ten to join their so-called army. To support their hungry militia, mainly Pakistanis and Arabs, they wanted all the crops of the year from all of our villagers. During these five years of their regime we had had no other income but our crops. We were alive because we grew some useful staples: wheat, rice, corn, potatoes and so on and ate what we grew. This announcement was a death sentence, not for one but for every villager at once. Some elders like uncle Rahim tried to argue with Mullah Jamil but the mullah drove the butt of a Kalashnikov into his chest, knocking the air out of him. We were accused of not being true Muslims because true Muslims gave everything to Allah.

We went back home aggrieved. I asked my father what he thought we should do. He said, "Don't worry; Allah is great. He will find a solution." I went out of the house and sat near the wheat we had recently harvested. I picked a few of those grains, positioned them on my palm, and thought in a few days we would have none of it. I shouted at the air, "God! Are you listening to us? Look what is happening. Will you take everything from us? Is this your justice? Are we only punished because we are born here and have no help?" I stretched out on the grass and fell asleep for some hours.

Ahmadshah woke me up. We went to the mosque. Almost every member of the village was there. Mullah Jamil made a list of male members over the age of ten. And he also ordered the amount of wheat, corn, and other grains that we were supposed to give to the government as soon as they returned for it. We all accepted their orders with no objection. At home we filled our bags with grain for the Taliban and hoped that some would be left for our survival. Mullah Jamil came with four large trucks and a few pickups, their white flags snapping in the wind. They put all the labor of our year on their trucks. Men stood there helplessly trying to forget the year of cultivation that came before and the year of hunger that would inevitably ensue.

Fahim's mother ran towards their vehicles and begged them not to take their grain because my uncle had a small farm. Mullah Jamil kicked her and said, "Crazy lady! God has given you a chance to prove that you are able to sacrifice everything you have for him and his cause."

My father murmured, "I do not know which God you are talking about. We know only Allah who is merciful and is always just. We will leave you to his hands."

I hugged my father and said, "Everything is going to be fine." All those trucks loaded with our crops moved toward Kabul. For almost half a mile, children ran after them, the Taliban throwing grains here or there from the open windows, a last taunt, or the genuine fullness of their generosity. My father and his brother sat together and put their hands on their foreheads like beggars, the sun already unsparing. I moved to the west side of the mosque where Ahmadshah and Fahim were sitting. I heard them talking about ways to get out of Afghanistan, to be smuggled or even to walk to Europe. The mountains had never seemed so impassable. They stood up like the flat brown seals of envelopes, one behind the other. Later on, all of us went to our homes. For a few hours there was complete silence in the village. We had nothing to say to each other in our house. That night we went to sleep at about six in the evening, exhausted. Actually we did not sleep, but remained in a darkness we thought would not pass.

# ICE CREAM

## HOSAI WARDAK

Furious with my mother, I look for my misplaced left sneaker among my expensive boots, fancy heels.

"Where is my shoe?" I call out in frustration.

My baby sister walks lopsided out of her room wearing my size 6-and-a-half Converse on her left foot. She trips while cheerfully saying, "Here it is." I take the shoe and stuff my foot in it. My mom and my joyful sister fix my baby sister's jacket before we walk out the door.

Living on the fourth floor of Macroryan, the apartment houses built by the Soviets in the 1960s, we had about seventy stairs to walk down before we would arrive at the front of our building. Our neighbors are not what my mother would refer to as *civilized people*. They have more kids living under one roof than a public elementary school. The mothers standing in the doorway call out after them, but they are always running up and down the stairs with candy and junk food in their hands, swearing at each other. They leave wrappers on the stairs and I kick them away like sticky leaves. The kids leave fingerprints on the doors, the walls, and the staircase railings. The younger females mostly have bright green, traditional Afghan baggy pants on, making me feel conspicuous in my skinny jeans.

While there, I am accosted by the odor of food being cooked for dinner rising out of the first floor windows, fried carrots and raisins. The scent of Pulao mixes with the smell of the trash-cans gathered in front of the apartment building. The scent is so strong from cooking oils that my sinuses burn. I see my baby sister with a bright smile on her face as she looks up at the sky and hears a helicopter flying overhead.

"Mama, when will we get on a plane again?" she asks.

My mother, not quite sure how to answer, avoids. "That's a helicopter for the Americans. What flavor ice cream do you want?" This is enough for my sister. She jumps up and down screaming, "Chocolate!" over and over.

We had returned to Kabul from Peshawar only six months earlier, and my sister's question was one that I had stopped asking my mother. Listening to my mother prevaricate, I no longer pay attention to her and make sure my bangs are fully covered by my scarf.

As we get farther away from the odors of the building and closer to the women's park, located between numerous Russian compounds, the smell of the newly watered juniper and conifer bushes replace the cramped domestic smells with wild and veg-etative ones. The park is set aside within these unlit bushes. The women gather where the moonlight is brightest; and wherever light cannot penetrate they do not go. Frequently, there are as many as fifty women gathered there at a time, speaking a wom-en's language unheard by men in this country.

Right across the park there is a mobile ice cream shop, outfit-ted with vivid pink and white globular lights. All four of us walk towards the shop, surrounded by mostly male hawkers, some with stupid comments on their lips for the women who enter or leave the park. We make our way into the crowd to order an ice cream and the men part to provide us space. After getting my ice cream, I overhear a man in his mid-thirties barking out something about my jeans, how disrespectful I am to wear them. Before I can even form the thought *disrespectful to what?* another, younger man argues with him, and my jeans evolve into a larger question about the politics in the country and Western influence in the world. My mother gives me a sharp, knowing look, having warned me before, then gets in front of them, excusing us all so that we can cut our way through the crowd. I can feel many men who fake a bump into me and then whisper their apology. It's exactly their hypocrisy that makes me feel entitled, even bold, about wearing the jeans, though I would never say this to my mother. The men's behavior, at once lewd and cowardly, disgusts me.

All the branches that encircle the park appear to be recently trimmed. I can't see a single leaf sticking out of its perfectly rectangular perimeter. Almost every ten feet, there are benches and small trashcans beside them. I like how the cans plea to be used, though ice cream wrappers decorate the path. My mother and sisters are investigating a convenient place to sit. Meanwhile, my baby sister releases my hand and quickens her pace. Pointing in the direction of a group of women who are now standing in black hijabs and blue chadris, she screams, "That bench is going to be free! They're leaving!"

I growl at her and ask if she could find a worse place to sit. Not catching my sarcasm my baby sister, confused, asks, "Why do you want to sit in a worse place?"

I ignore her. She's found the one place where the scruffy boys peek in through the bushes. My mother and my two sisters seem to be relishing the shadows that crowd around our feet and crawl onto our laps. Everyone appears to be doing their own thing except—like typical Afghans—they are all eavesdropping on each other's conversations. And so are we.

"Mom, did you ever imagine we would have segregated parks just so we could safely get an ice cream at night when you were growing up here?"

She sighed. "We don't have kings any more. What do you expect from democracy?" My mother infrequently spoke of the time of Afghanistan's last king, as though nostalgia for that period of Afghan manners that she knew from her mother's recounting, could never be restored to the wild people who now controlled everything.

A girl and an elderly woman, who seems to be her mother, are sitting together on a rickety bench nearby, sharing a large cup of ice cream. I squint my eyes to see their activity and it reminds me of Renoir's painting *Le Moulin de la Galette,* a painting we discussed in my Art and Civilization class at a private school in Pakistan. Other ladies, passing by, are scrutinizing me head to toe like I'm of a different gender, not quite male or female. I forget how much this is a culture easily confused by disguise; gender is simply what you wear.

The tag inside my pink H&M shrug is digging into my neck. I am too lazy to go back home to change. My hands are tired of trying to pull out the tightly stitched label; I am too concerned about how to avoid making a hole in my favorite jacket by ripping it off "uncivilly" or in an "unladylike" way, as my mother would put it.

Two creepy ladies who have remained behind, relinquishing this bench briefly when their other friends left, scowl at us for taking the bench from them. They take a seat on the bench behind us and turn around like loose screws to watch us. My mother, enjoying a good conversation with our neighbor, doesn't notice the stares my sisters and I have been receiving.

As I take a spoonful of ice cream, I zone out in the still beauty of the oncoming darkness that obliterates the outlines of the ugly apartments. I realize the power of darkness, of concealment; the effect it can have on a city like Kabul, a place where looking at the wrong man too long or too critically can cause problems. A little kid carrying two cups of ice cream on a tray blocks my view for a second as he passes in front of me. Young boys are allowed in here, as though they don't possess a gender until puberty, or until a woman disapproves of their presence. My eyes follow him as he hands over two cups of ice cream to the shrouded ladies sitting behind me. I lick my spoon clean and shovel the inedible old nuts onto the dirt near the tree roots; I imagine them growing into trees of their own. Before my mind can drift off again, the women's voices rise amidst a high giggle. "Yeah, these people who come from *kharej* (a foreign country), trying to modernize our culture, they are a disgrace to the Afghan society," says one of the women, sitting behind me, but speaking loud enough, obviously intending it for me.

I couldn't resist but to turn around and look at the same time she did. Neither of us felt ashamed as our eyes met.

Shaking my head in contempt, I say to my sister, "Good God, the combination of hijab and the gothic eye make-up makes her look like a Holloween ghoul." My middle sister chuckles and gives them a mocking look through the corner of her glasses before she gets up to push our baby sister on the swingset.

It is itchy. I feel like the tag will give me blisters if I don't take it off in the next minutes. I choose to tuck my scarf inside my jacket so that the tag doesn't irritate my skin even though the scarf no longer fully covers my head. The lady with the eye make-up sounds different now. I can hear her making comments on the inappropriate attire of other women in the park. From behind the tree, I hear my baby sister calling, "push me higher," and my other sister obliging her.

I am hoping the ladies are done yapping about random things but for a strange reason I still lean back on the bench and pretend to look at the sky, just so I can hear them better. The one with the Goth make-up says, "If the Americans are really leaving, why don't these newcomers go with them."

After some whispering, I hear the lady in the sky-blue chadri say, "These shameless girls and newcomers. Tempting our men. We don't need them corrupting our society. They don't belong here anymore."

I take a spoonful of ice cream and feel it freeze the back of my throat. I think for a moment of my mother, who has gone walking with the neighbor. Will she earn the acceptance of these women having returned back to her homeland, and what will she have to do to maintain it? The tag that irritates my neck doesn't compare to the level of annoyance these women feel just seeing me in clothing made elsewhere: in China, India, Bangladesh, Vietnam—wherever women sewed it. And probably, women in hijab here will soon manufacture these same clothes in Kabul. If we stay at peace—or in this war that maintains some level of peace—then we'll all be doing piecework together. Otherwise, hijab or not, no one will be Afghan enough for this country, no one non-Western enough.

The lady with the Goth make-up spits to her right.

At that moment, a sound of the branches crunching makes all of us turn in the direction of the park's perimeter. A skinny teenage boy with bad acne falls through the hedges onto the path. He scrambles to pick himself up and slip through the bushes that have tightly closed behind him. It's clear he'll cut himself up badly trying to scuttle away from us. We can hear his friend laughing behind him. "Mirwais! Are you trying to serve them ice cream or are you putting on a show?"

Judging by where he's fallen, he was trying to get a glimpse of the two covered women, though I'm unsure they're smart enough to recognize this, or if their propriety makes it impossible for them to accept it. They gasp and quickly cover themselves; it seems they understand and appreciate their own corrupting influence.

I turn around to the poor kid. He's mostly disappeared now into the bramble. "Why not take a long look now that you've revealed yourself," I call out. The entire scene seems silly. My provocative entreaty has the other women fleeing. I can't hear them above the sound of helicopters returning to their bases.

My mother and sisters have come back. They pull my hand. "We have to get home now. Your father is bringing one of his colleagues from Pakistan and we have to prepare dinner."

I keep looking back. Other ladies are exiting the park, as though we were their only entertainment that night. They grow dimmer in the darkness, moving out in separate directions. On my way home, I hold my mother's arm and my baby sister's hand, thinking that whatever my father's friend sees of this country, it won't be the same country my mother and sisters live in.

# THE SNOW OVER THE STONES
## ZAHRA KHAWARI

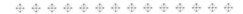

You are the only one who knows the truth. I don't want to continue. You were so young. A child…

I had to keep that job. I didn't know why I was going to that damn office to hear my boss bellowing, "You're late again. You're fired! Get out now!"

Your voice that morning shook me out of my reverie. "Mom! Mom!" I quickly took the corner of my scarf and wiped my eyes.

"Yes, my dear? Why did you wake up so early?"

"I… I… want to say, don't forget to have your lunch! Otherwise you will faint like last night. And take these gloves! I borrowed them from aunt Lila." Even as a child, you wanted to take care of me.

I told you, "But I have mine, give them back to her. Go on, she's only next door." I smiled at her, "This time, I won't forget to bring you new gloves! Now go home, it is very cold outside; you did not put your scarf and socks on. I will count to ten and you should be with your grandmother. Make sure you kiss her and oil her feet."

"But Mom!" You did not want to be without me, and I could barely bring myself to leave.

"One, two, three, four… don't run! It's icy everywhere!"

I exhaled cold smoke and released a deep sigh. I closed the gate. The roads were empty; there was nothing except the white cover of snow over stones and mud. There weren't any cars on the main road, so I walked faster. I knew it would be easier to get a taxi. Money *is* important too; I have to save it from now on. There would be more than a few challenging roads to walk. I didn't care, even if the roads were empty, the snow was heavy, the wind was sharp, and hungry dogs were looking for food. Dogs, I do not like them!

My life is worse than theirs. At least the dogs might get a fair shake. That's what I remember thinking.

I walked for almost fifteen minutes before I approached the narrow, kinky roads of Mahal-e-Wardaka. The snow slowed my progress; I couldn't see the potholes in the sidewalk. Still, I would not stop. I had to learn to like these long walks. I knew the sun would make tomorrow's walk much harder, that the streets would swim with mud.

Why couldn't I breathe properly? Why was my heart beating so fast? At first, I worried it was another fainting spell. Why was the screaming so clear, outside of me? Where was she?

The gate in front of the impoverished house was half open. As the screams grew louder, I instinctively pushed it wide. I could not believe what I was looking at. She was in flames, running back and forth in the yard. Her screams cut through me. At first, I was too shocked to react. I looked around the yard to find something to put out the fire, but the yard was messy, wash-tubs sunk unevenly in the snow and dresses strewn about. By the doorway a thin tree had been used for hanging the wet, frozen clothes. The house was very old. There were two plain windows beside the entrance door. I saw a man with a black mustache and beard looking through the window. He stepped back into the darkness, a figure that preferred the shadows. I ran toward the door, enraged, and banged on it. The door was locked. I took off my gloves and was pummeling the door with both my red fists and shouting for help. But nobody came out. Even the neighbors, despite my screaming, would not dare come out.

She was a fireball. I had to stop it. I saw the buckets of gray water near the gate. She must have been a washerwoman. I ran towards them, but I remembered water is not the best way to put out a fire. I tried to find other things in the yard. I saw the old blanket that hung in front of the door, used as a thick curtain to keep the cold air outside. I ripped it down and covered the girl with it. I made her lie on the ground. She didn't scream anymore, just murmured and whimpered. I was trembling the whole time. What should I do next? I ran to the door again, knocked on it and yelled for help. I returned to her.

*What the hell was this world so silent about? Had fear stuffed our mouths with cotton?*

I covered her in the blanket. Was there another way? She was dying. I called my friend who works as a nurse in Herat's main hospital. Then I leaned over to look at the girl, moving the blanket carefully from her face. By now she was completely quiet; her eyes were open, staring at some blind point in the sky. Her features were burned and her eyelashes and eyebrows gone. Her face was mottled, red meat. I didn't dare ask myself any questions. I wanted to comfort her, but I was afraid she would speak. I wanted her to remain mute; any sound would have been too painful.

I imagine she was around twenty, very young. She was like crumpled wastepaper on the ground. When I tried to take the blanket away from her, she gave me a cold but weak look. Tears came to her eyes.

When I heard the ambulance, I ran toward the gate to direct them. I suspect I could no longer bear seeing her. I showed them the way. They took her to the ambulance. Without any questioning I got in and sat close to her. She started murmuring. She didn't feel pain, although I later learned she was burned over eighty-five percent of her body. Her murmurings suggested something very important…but why? Was she worrying about a child at home? The way I worried about you? *She must have wanted this. She must have done this to make a point.*

Unthinkable.

*– Did she really want this?*

They took her to the ICU. I didn't have the energy to move and sat quietly behind the operating room door. I leaned my head back on the wall. Was I tired? No. I was thinking how late I would be for work. How horrible to think about work while someone is dying.

Nurses and doctors passed me by, barely a look. I was watching them in silence. An old woman who seemed to be one of the patients' visitors came to me and said, "What is your relationship with her? Are you her teacher?" I just stared at her. She asked, "Why did she do this?" I hated being asked that question. Because I knew what had driven her.

"I don't know why!" I practically hollered. "I don't know her." We turned to the nurse who was standing with an old woman, her burkha lifted, revealing her wizened face. The nurse pointed at me and then at the old woman. Then she vanished.

The old woman came toward me. I stood up. Our eyes met in sorrow. She cried in silence and shook her head. She leaned on the wall, sat, and kept her head between her hands. "He killed her. He didn't want her anymore. His brothers… She wasn't able to bring enough money to that house. You know why? She was beaten. She didn't have the energy to wash the neighbors' clothes. Her husband's family didn't give her and her child food. She worked a lot, but it was her duty to pay for her child and her husband's opium." She leaned back and continued to cry louder, murmuring to herself, "My flower, my daughter, my Raihan. Forgive your mother for what she couldn't do for you!"

I wanted to take her hand, but didn't. I had to get to work. I left her to her grief, alone.

You do understand. I had to get to work. Money was important. I had to keep my job so that you could have a chance, so that you could get a fair shake. I never mentioned it to anyone. I waited until you were old enough, until you understood what it meant to be a woman.

# TEN SHOTGUNS

## NAJIBULLAH NAQIB

✳ ✳ ✳ ✳ ✳ ✳ ✳ ✳ ✳ ✳ ✳ ✳ ✳ ✳

I am lying on my roof at the very silent corner of my yard in a village in northeastern Afghanistan. The familiar constellations are very clear, as though the most important things in life were happening out there. I reach out to turn off the kerosene lamp that illuminates the surface of my sleeping bag. My grandson, Makamtash, approaches me. He is a hard-headed man in his early twenties. He was a handsome boy, even exceptionally so, but now it is apparent that life has offered little that he expected and disappointment has already begun to haunt his face. He attended many of the religious lessons in our village mosque and is the only one in our family who can read and write. His religious teacher had encouraged him to enroll in the district school and continue his education. He implored me to let him attend, but I opposed him and his mother. Now, I am so remorseful and feel accountable, at least toward him.

These days he is of great assistance to me, chiefly because of his literacy and familiarity with modern ways. He accompanies me to all the local councils and reads the petitions and documents of the local villagers who have cases, different disputes, and helps me to make my final decisions. Although he has grown up with his father and uncles, who have always had a great love for brand new Kalashnikovs, he has never touched one and sometimes I see him helping his mother and other aunts with the household drudgeries. His father always calls him *zancha*, or one who has lost his manhood because of his good relations with the women of the household.

He looks at me and gently says, "Grandma, dinner is ready and we are waiting for you."

"Son, you may go, I will follow you shortly," I reply. Sleep has become a habit. The normal schedule of the family is no longer of interest to me.

We are twenty-eight people in the household and all the meals are eaten in the living room. My daughters-in-law roll out a long black cotton cloth on the floor to make sure everyone has a space and then they bring enough bread and food and serve all the male members of the family and me first. The women always feel daunted when I enter the living room and this is because I have sacrificed my femaleness by carrying arms and fighting for them.

After a few moments I go down to join the others. Weariness has earned a place in this room. Everything has been polished, washed, sat on, used and scrubbed too often. All pretenses of success, except survival itself, have long since vanished from its atmosphere. Moreover, a section of the room slopes under the weight of my weapons and ammunitions cache. Our house is very big and, located—nest-like—amid barren crags. Several other houses, each with a varying lack of distinction—as though distinction itself were something too precious here—constitutes the community. The village's only feature now is that it has clearly accommodated too many people for too many years. It's rundown.

By today's standards, our village is a primitive place. There are no health facilities or remaining schools. A dirt road runs down to the creek where women and children are sent for fresh water, and the hubub of their activity goes on throughout the day. The creek is also a source of conflict and misery during the years of drought and water shortage. Sometimes when there is a shortage, I dispatch a group of my armed men to safeguard our supply from the strongmen of the village. Another dirt road meanders off toward the center of our district, Hazarsumech, and it takes us four hours by donkeys and mules to visit a doctor or exchange goods on market days in the bazaar.

A long time ago I married a man in whose shadow I still continue to live. I knew him from the days of my childhood because he made boots for my father and brothers; he inhabited, with his elder brother, two little connected shops in the bazaar. He was a young man, full-bodied and strong. He was one of those men of a certain grace and handsomeness that wore it so unobtrusively it took a while to notice. His pale face was surrounded with his black and wild hair, and his features were angular and deep-set, as though a sculptor had chiseled them with certainty. Like most other Afghans who have no family name, he went by only one, Peermad.

On market days, when my father took us to the bazaar, we would surely pay a visit to him and my father would ask me to stay in his shop until he finished buying what we needed. Sometimes Peermad would offer to take me to other shops and buy me fake bracelets and rings, things that didn't threaten my father, but that hid a budding courtship between us. We started to love each other from those intermittent meetings. After four years, when I was just sixteen, his family proposed and my father accepted our marriage, provided that Peermad would live in our house. We had children and led a happy life for the first few years.

I vividly remember when the Kingdom collapsed in a coup orchestrated by the king's cousin. I heard the word *Republic* for the first time at a gathering in our village and asking Peermad what it meant. He said it meant we would have a share in the government. After a few years, this government also crumbled from within by a communist takeover. Soon after its installment, the new regime had begun indoctrinating students and farmers in different districts with communist dogma, offering incentives and political support. In our district, the teacher and farmer cooperatives had recruited many locals into the People's Democratic Party of Afghanistan and all the members were provided with red ID cards and badges that indicated their conviction. They believed that the resources of the nation would be equally distributed among its citizens.

The district governor had tried to enforce new regulations on land reforms and family issues that were heavily criticized by religious and tribal leaders. In response to the new regulations, there was a terrible riot in the bazaar. The governor's security personnel had attacked the rioters and as a result many people were killed and injured. Then the rioters had overpowered and killed the district governor and most of his security. Peermad's brother was also killed. It was midnight and I was asleep on a makeshift bed at the center of the living room. My older son, Qujqar, gave me a rousing shake and said, "Mama, somebody is knocking on the door very loudly."

I stood up and sleepily crossed toward the window. I caught a glimpse of what was happening. I found many villagers had huddled together in front of our gate.

"Hurry up and inform your uncles," I told Qujqar. My brothers opened the gate and my husband, with a lot of other villagers who carried his brother's body, entered our yard. In the history of the village—at least from what was recounted by our grandfathers—it was the first time that the government had dealt such a blow to our people. We counted nine of our villagers among thirty-eight people killed on that day.

My husband came into the living room. He cried, leaned his head back and said, "It seems that God didn't see fit to bring us anything but misery. The communists are giving people's land away, stealing their property. They are even controlling our marriages."

The next morning, all the men of the village were invited to the mosque for the funeral ceremony and after an interminable speech that made everyone cry, the mullah told the villagers that this was an act of aggression by a godless regime and declared jihad against it. The nine bodies were buried on the top of a hill about three hundred meters away from our house and after a few days their cemetery became a shrine. The mullah had a dream that virginal angels had married all nine men.

Almost a week later, one of our villagers who had come from the capital of the district informed the mullah and the elders of the village that the communist government had retaliated by sending army tanks and military personnel into the district to suppress those who had orchestrated the riot that resulted in the murder of the district governor and the policemen. I remember it was the middle of November and I was collecting leaves for fuel with the other women of the village. At that time the other women were not afraid of me. I was one of them. It was just a month after the riot, when we heard shooting and the commands of the KHAD, the Afghan secret police in the village.

My father entered the house and asked, "Where are Peermad and your brothers?"

"Samay and Raziq are at home, but Peermad and the others are on the farm," I answered.

"Get your children inside the bunker and inform your brothers not to go out because the police are arresting everyone indiscriminately," he said.

"What is happening father? Why are they shooting?"

"Those were just warning shots. Don't be alarmed. Somebody tried to escape," he said.

He looked around and started walking toward the toilet, where he would frequently go to smoke when he was worried. I heard him latch the wooden door. I took all the children inside the bunker where we had piled our rugs and other things for the winter.

By the time I came out, a crowd of policemen had gathered in front our house and one of them shouted, "Ask your men to come out of the house or we will get them out. Do you hear me? I am asking all the men to come out of this house," he insisted.

My father told my brothers to use the ladder in the backyard, and run through our garden to our neighbor's house. They could not make it. The policemen entered our house and one of them, a tall man with a thick mustache, got close to my father and slapped him. He ordered the other policemen to tie my brothers' and father's hands. We started crying and I went to resist the policemen but one of them cussed at me and hit me on the back with his gun and said, "Do not get closer or I'll shoot you right here."

"Where are you taking my father and brothers, they have done nothing," I said.

"Don't worry, we will ask them some questions and let them return home," one of the policemen said.

They arrested fifteen people in our village that day, including the mullah, my father and brothers, and some others who visited the district capital regularly. No one saw them again. At sunset my husband and my two other brothers, Satar and Wali, came home. As dusk deepened, the stillness resettled, and we could barely bring ourselves to speak. Later in the night, my husband and brothers went out of the house and mobilized more than fifty men in the village to take up arms and resist the KHAD. They knew that those arrested would be killed. They had collected some ten shotguns from different families in the village. Peermad had proposed to the villagers that he would start patrolling overnight and during the day, and the ten shotguns could be kept at our home. Some men of the village dared to travel to the center of the district to obtain more arms and ammunition. I don't know what got into me—perhaps seeing my husband's despair at the loss of his brother, or having seen my father slapped and taken from me—but I asked Peermad if I, too, could carry a shotgun. He laughed as he used to when I was just a child in his shop asking for more jewelry.

"You can be the lookout," he consented warmly. Then he sent me to the roof of our house where, to this day, I still watch the night sky.

The rising dust along the road from the mountains signaled an approaching car. I shouted a warning that the police were coming. People emerged from their houses. Guesses were hazarded about how many cars the dust cloud might obscure. Then— a big moment in the day—the ten shotguns were distributed, people disappeared, and by this time Peermad had taken the role of planner and commander.

"How many are they?" Peermad asked me.

"I can't get a good look. It looks like about five."

Then, after the dust cleared slightly, I told him, "It's a Russian Jeep and contains five."

"Hold your positions and two of you should take one of them from a closer distance when they stop," Peermad ordered his men. "Do it from a closer distance or we will not have the pleasure of testing these nice Russian guns on their makers."

I watched the men fan out from our property and then from our rooftop I shouted, "Shoot them!" The five of them were killed. I may have been the only person in the position to see all five of them die.

On that day, the village savored the fruits of a victory that had much harsher repercussions. Five KHAD policemen were killed and their bodies were dragged to different locations and beaten spontaneously by the villagers. The village gunners availed themselves of five Kalashnikovs, three pistols and twenty-five hand grenades that they took from the dead. The excitement of our vengeance prevailed in our family and the village for weeks. In the glow of that victory, Peermad began to take me out privately and taught me to shoot. I loved it, each cloud of dust after a target shattered.

One evening my husband came home. He was tired, worried, and he spoke with reticence. He softly murmured, "Can I talk to you for a minute?"

"Yes, of course," I replied.

"The village is no longer safe. We have decided that the women and children should be taken to the summer shelters."[1]

---

1. Summer shelters are temporary rooms built by different villagers on the grasslands in the mountains. They live there during summer when they take their herds of livestock to the pasturelands.

"Winter is approaching. It will be hard to live in those cold areas," I explained.

"We have no other alternative," he said as he started to leave.

"When will you come back?" I asked.

"Tomorrow morning, but Wali will stay with you tonight," he said.

It was early in the morning. My sister and I went to the kitchen to prepare breakfast. As we entered the kitchen, we heard a lot of noise, firing and the rumbling of vehicles. We rushed to the room and took the children into the bunker. My sister went to Wali's room but he had already left the house. For a few minutes, my sister and I felt abandoned and wept but I assured my children that nothing would happen. The firing continued for almost half an hour and then it stopped. A group of almost twenty policemen were led to our house. They started searching the rooms and we could clearly hear their footsteps and voices. Some of them spoke in a foreign language. They finally found their way into the bunker. Everyone was frightened and crying. One of them, who looked as if he was their commander, stared at my sister and said in our language, Uzbec, "Don't be afraid, we have some questions to ask you regarding the attack yesterday."

I pleaded for their mercy. "Sir, all of you have sisters and mothers, we are innocent." Even as I said this, I imagined shooting him, the pleasure of seeing his blood.

"Take the ladies outside of the bunker, one of you should stay with the children," he said.

They did not ask any questions. Instead, they took us to the yard. It was a shockingly clear, sunny day. The snow was like a thin blue glass over the ground. Their commander approached my sister. He started to touch her breasts and then he kissed her.

I yelled and cussed at them but I could not move because two policemen were holding me. We were imploring for help and the whole village could hear us, but no one came to defend us. He yanked my sister down, took off her clothes and tried to rape her but she resisted. She was stark naked in front of all the policemen. They stood by laughing. He punched her in the face and then asked his men to hold her for him. She was shouting and asking for help and swearing at them. After the commander's sexual desire was met, he shot her and walked off.

Then it was my turn. Six policemen dragged me back into the house and into the bedroom. The children were crying in the bunker as they heard my screaming. I was struggling, resisting and hollering, but two of them grabbed my legs firmly and the others took off my clothes. They raped me individually and one by one left the room. I was so powerless, I could not move. I was lying naked on the floor of the bedroom. There was another stocky, blonde policeman. I thought he was as stupid and bland as a large bundle of wheat, and I closed my eyes not to see him. He thought that I was unconscious and put his gun next to me. I fully submitted to his desires and did not move. I felt excruciating pain as he penetrated me but I tried not to flinch. When he finished, he stood up to tie his pants. I grabbed his gun and holding it with both hands, pointed it at his head. He tried to warn me he had a hand grenade on his waist, but I pulled the trigger. Other policemen who were in the yard thought their comrade had killed me. My whole body was trembling, but I managed to crawl closer to the window.

One of the policemen tried to look inside the room but as he came closer, I fired at his chest. The others started firing at the window and they were shouting, fearing they were ambushed and were informing the other policemen that the *basmachs*, insurgents, had infiltrated the house. But it was only I against them, determined to spill the blood of every one of them. They started running out of the house as I fired the last bullets remaining in the magazine of my gun. Having been stripped of my own, I immediately put on my husband's clothes and since then I have never worn women's clothes again. After almost half an hour, I heard firing and the voices of village men who were calling, "God is great! God is great!" I understood that the bastards were defeated. I was completely paranoid and took the Kalashnikovs from the dead and fired repeatedly at our gate. The exchange of fire continued in the village for at least an hour. Then the stillness returned.

I ran toward my sister, Raheela. She was still naked and her face was smeared with blood. She was barely recognizable. She was twenty, as slim and intense as her father. She was not as pretty as our mother, but her lean, almost intellectual face had a handsomeness of its own. That morning she wore a bright-red flannel dress that our village tailor had made for her. I was not bold enough to touch her, but I covered her with a long cloth. I ran down to the bunker and my children ran toward me and they hugged me. All the children were terrified of the shooting.

On that day, my husband and brothers came home at noon. They already knew what had happened. All of them were crying. My husband ran to the bunker. He hugged the children and me. I had never seen him cry like our own children. My two brothers fainted when they saw the naked body of our sister. Somebody in the village had led the policemen to all the houses of those villagers who had participated in the attack on the KHAD personnel and their wives, sisters, and female relatives were all raped. It was not only our family that cracked under the strain of this grief.

The ten villagers, under the command of my husband, had also dealt a blow to the policemen. First they were overpowered and fled from the center of the village but later they used each bullet at their disposal and attacked from different positions. As a result, almost nine policemen were killed outside of our house. The routine of those days was shaped by tragedy. After that incident, the villagers started to live in harmony, quarrels and rivalries were put aside.

All the village elders, including my husband and brothers, appreciated my courage for taking my sister's revenge. I also became one of the village fighters. They took the bodies of the policemen out of our house and we buried my sister the next day. By this time, twenty-five villagers were armed. My husband had also seized an RPG with thirteen grenades. The KHAD tried in vain to attack the village overnight and for some reason they stopped riding in their armored vehicles.

For many nights, my husband and I, our brothers and other villagers, would go to different locations near the only outlet to the district and we would wait for the KHAD to come but they wouldn't arrive. On one snowy night, we decided to ambush them in a graveyard that was located next to the road five kilometers away from our village. I came up with a plan that evening. I told my husband and the group that we should wear white clothes and paint our guns white because it had snowed for a couple of days and it would be easy to disguise ourselves. We walked for an hour and a half until we reached that graveyard. All of us settled behind a grave and waited for the KHAD. It was freezing. We waited until midnight but they did not show up. Just as we started to go back to the village, we heard someone singing.

The whole group returned to their positions and we saw a line of policemen walking along the road toward the village. As they got closer, my husband ordered the group to hold their fire. They were a distance of fifteen meters from us. My husband stood up and shouted, Allah-u-akbar. Then every one of us opened fire on them. One of the police shot Peermad and he collapsed. After we exchanged fire for fifteen minutes, they stopped shooting and were screaming that they surrendered. As I stood beside Peermad's body, I commanded the men to capture the nine policemen with their commander. Around seventeen were killed in our ambush.

My fighters dug the grave for my husband and we buried him beside my sister. In a matter of years, I led a contingent of 150 men. I looked at none of them. Just as I had rid myself of women's clothes, I had closed myself off to women's desires. I understood those men; I had nothing—no passion in my heart but vengeance.

Thirty years have gone by. Yes, the sun has come over the mountains thousands of times. Summers and winters have cracked the mountains a little bit more and the rains have brought down tragedies but also prosperity. Most of the babies in our family that weren't even born at that time have begun lecturing on a myriad of subjects, including the roles of men and women under Islam. They don't lecture me, though. A number of people who thought that they were young and spry have noticed they can't bound up a flight of stairs as they used to. I rely on my grandson to take me to the rooftops when the days are sunny, when visitors kick up their clouds of dust, and he and I read the landscape together.

# THE TASTE OF CAKE

## AHMAD RESHAD MAJIDI

❋ ❋ ❋ ❋ ❋ ❋ ❋ ❋ ❋ ❋ ❋ ❋ ❋

Sergeant Eskandari says, "Happy birthday, son."

Ali dares to move his eyes and look at the Sergeant's face while his mouth is open, about to suck, his nose filled with the smell of the Sergeant's crotch. At least the Sergeant's face is tolerable. His face is freshly shaved and does not have the long hair that surrounds his penis.

Tonight Ali cannot do it. Not because he is not good at it, but because this has been the only task he has been allowed to be good at, and he would like to show the Sergeant that he can do other things. The Sergeant is nice enough to understand him and not feed him his urine. After all he has a son with a birthday this same week, a son who is studying for a medical university pre-test.

Ali hears the voice and footsteps of soldier Rahimi. They get louder as he moves closer. He is here. Thank god. Delay.

"It's prayer time sir, the brothers are waiting for you," the young soldier says, looking at the worn, ill-fitting Afghan clothes on Ali's underfed body.

"Yes, OK, Rahimi. I am almost finished with this one. He's no good tonight anyway," the Sergeant says after spitting paan on the floor.

"Anything else, soldier? Heard me?" Sergeant Eskandari is not interested in the soldier's answers, wants him gone.

Ali half-heartedly begins performing the task while listening to the footsteps move down the hall. Eskandari shoves Ali's head back. "Useless," he says.

As Ali lifts himself from the floor, wiping the dirt from his knees, the sergeant speaks to him. "Clean yourself up. Sleep well son, tomorrow after prayer you will get what you were waiting for."

Eskandari pulls up his dark green pants, a costume different from the other Sergeants around the country. Everything is different in Zahedan from other Iranian towns, except maybe its prisons. It's a Sunni border town, and the language is Baluchi. Ali could not understand the soldier who picked him up for drug smuggling three years earlier. He still does not know what he was charged for or how long he'll remain under the Sergeant's care.

The Sergeant, holding the back of his neck, brings Ali to a new cell, this one with a clock. It shows 11:30 pm. Its tic-tocks are clear and loud, a reminder of the dull moments that pass in the mostly soundless prison.

Tonight Ali is one of the only ones given the chance to know what the time is. The numbers are some kind of incomprehensible gift from the Sergeant. Ali had never encountered numbers in his childhood. Even his birthday comes inexplicably. Soldier Rahimi told him that tomorrow would be a special day, celebrated with cake and balloons, but of course, Ali remembers only the condoms that the Taliban used as balloons. They were not so special, not colorful.

Though Ali does not know numbers, he knows that seeing the clock is part of his gift. The clock must be worth a lot of money; it has Tom and Jerry on it. He had last seen that cartoon when the smuggler had given him the brick to put in his backpack. The smuggler was watching it on a black-and-white TV and Ali's face had contorted in silent laughter as the cat and mouse hit each other with a frying pan.

Maybe there's an expensive clock in every hell and maybe they also welcome the new arrivals with a boiling shower, as they had done with Ali. He had been sorted with the women and kids for special purposes. He was told he was special for the first time, and though they were rough with him, he believed it.

The Sergeant is gone. Ali cannot sleep. It is like the first time he slept in this shelter. He thought of his mother, and how she'd made him sleep outside with their donkey. She told him he was illegitimate, and that's why he was mute, so he could keep her secret. That wasn't enough. When he was fourteen, they rode the donkey from their village into Zabul where she left him in a vegetable market. He waited for three days, hungry and cold, stealing carrots. That's when the man invited him to come and watch cartoons, then paid his way to Zahedan, putting the brick into his otherwise empty backpack.

When the soldiers check him with flashlights, dark circles are visible around his eyes. They have been there since Sergeant Eskandari was transferred from Qom. It was last year. Sergeant Eskandari started using Ali's mouth as his ejaculating machine, reasoning a mouth has to do three tasks: breathe, eat and speak and since Ali cannot speak, it should be used for other purposes.

There is a problem with this clock, Ali thinks. Why do people look at them? There's a time to eat and pray and soldier Rahimi knows when these times are and tells everyone. What is the point of a clock, he wonders.

Soldier Rahimi and the executioners might be sleeping, but they are snoring in a vast part of the world that Ali knows nothing about. They'll wake up looking at their own clocks; they will wake up like normal people do. They will pray, have their breakfasts: hot sangak bread, fresh oregano, mint and cheese that would be prepared by their mothers. They will come to work, test the rope, clean their guns, and throw buckets of water onto the cell floors. They will wear their uniforms, cleaned of blood by their wives.

Ali has been waiting for his eighteenth birthday, as he is told other kids do. The Sergeant has told him that his own son will become a man today.

Ali's birthday and birthday gift were planned in 2004, three years ago. The court planned it after hearing nothing from him in his defense. They simply didn't care if he could speak or not, if he had a tongue or not. The case was already taking a long time and had to conclude. They fixed him a date of birth. It took clergy to decide that. The judge announced the sentence. Ali and his lawyer, who was busy thinking of another case, accepted the outcome.

It is not a normal day, like yesterday and the days before. A normal day begins with the smell of shit from the toilet at the end of the so-called Afghan hall, where the air conditioner system stopped working last year. Today there is no smell, no other Afghans whispering. It starts with Rahimi's footsteps in the hollow quiet that allows the clock to seem like it's speaking.

When Rahimi arrives, Ali jumps to his feet, expectant. Rahimi is grateful that Ali cannot ask for the cake, to ask stupid questions about what it would taste like, or what color the balloons in Iran are. Instead, he walks him down the hall, passing empty cells that reverberate in Rahimi's mind with pleading men who cried or fought or talked about seeing their needy wives and

children one last time, offered to do anything, to pay anything—
this from men with no money. Ali is smiling. He can see the light
around the gray door. It must be hundreds of candles. Perhaps
Eskandari will sing. Ali has heard him singing in the halls before. Rahimi opens the heavy gray door that leads to a sun-filled
courtyard. The buildings are gray except for spray-painted words
in Farsi and a chipped painting of Khomeini, over which blood is
sprayed. The ground too, is gray. The only green under the shaft
of sunlight is the uniforms worn by the soldiers lined against a
wall.

"Stand here," Rahimi tells Ali politely, and then he goes and
joins the other soldiers at the opposite wall. They lift their guns
at the same time. Rahimi has never seen someone so compliant.
Ali is standing, smiling ludicrously, as though this is his luckiest
day, as though no days had been lived before. Ali trusts Rahimi
to tell him when to sleep or pray, to suck or shit. Time, whether
we get more or less of it, means nothing.

# AGSHAR'S SECRET

## MOHEBULLAH FAGHIRI

❋ ❋ ❋ ❋ ❋ ❋ ❋ ❋ ❋ ❋ ❋ ❋ ❋

Shakib had no idea where he was walking that autumn day. The dried leaves fell from the trees and skittered around their trunks. He felt pain through his entire body, a faint, unfamiliar pain. Never had he imagined the harsh actions taken against his brothers, Ahmad and Hasib. But here he was, in the streets of Herat, only a couple of days after escaping from the Policharkhi Prison, with that cursed moment of gunshots still ringing in his ears. He wheeled around lost.

"Hey, watch your step!" said a peddler at the curb. "You were about to walk on my nail clippers!"

"I'm sorry," Shakib said.

"You seem miserable. Are you injured? Is there anything I can do for you?" His sympathy momentarily hung in the air between them, strange to hear; the country was at war and kindnesses were rare.

"No, thanks," Shakib glanced at him. "God will help me!"

*God will help me.* But how would God help him? He frequently heard from his father and all of his friends that their lives were in God's hands. His father was a martyred leader who suffered many hardships before his early death. Shakib, in a sustained state of dizziness, wondered what would become of him. From his upbringing, he too was religious, but now he felt like no one could bring his brothers back. *Not even God.*

He didn't realize how long he was walking or how long it would take to reach the station of minivans going to the Guzara district. His mother and little sisters along with his uncle had escaped to this desert village outside Herat in fear of the punishments the government would mete out. KHAD, the national security wing of the communist government, would not hesitate to kill or arrest them for the possession of anti-communist leaflets.

The Soviet army made their presence known through a series of desperate and brutal raids. Communism spread everywhere. Government officials were following the Khalq party's ideology. They were opposed to religious thought and practices. KHAD would destroy anyone standing before them. They entered the universities and high schools asking the students the question: *Khalqisti ya Musalman?* "Are you a Khalqi or a Muslim?" If the students said they were Khalqi, they would be freed. Otherwise, they would be arrested and executed. This was how Shakib's older brothers were arrested at Kabul Medical University.

Shakib entered a minivan and was pressed by strangers that made his bruised body ache even more. He remembered the algae crawling the humid walls of the prison cells, living fingerprints. The odor of spilled blood and urine hung in the air of the cell. Shakib was put into this cage with Asghar, who was also arrested because he would not identify as Khalqi. Shakib's brothers were in other cells. He had no idea what had happened to them. Perhaps they were shackled in cells close to his. He cried out their names. And then others began to call for family members. It sounded like a kennel of wounded animals.

"Does your family know that you were arrested?" Shakib asked Asghar solicitously. "They might be able to help you out of here."

There was a grave silence for a second or two. "No one knows I am here," said Asghar.

"Are you afraid?"

"Of course I am. I don't want to be here. I feel nauseous. The soldiers hit me on the head. It's bleeding badly." He parted his hair and showed a large crimson wound.

Shakib turned away. Though his father had hoped all his sons would go to medical school, Shakib sickened easily at the sight of blood. "You have to tolerate this, brother," he said, looking away. "God will help us. He hears us. He will bestow us blessings and mercy in heaven after we are martyred."

"I don't want to die. I am still too young. I have too many wishes and desires." Asghar's voice was trembling. His words seemed childish to Shakib. Though Shakib could understand Asghar's fear, he had been raised on the glories of martyrdom. It was his father who had taught him sacrifice. At only twenty-four years of age, he could bear such situations—*was created to bear them.* He sometimes thought that he was being tested after being chased and beaten by communist supporters.

The cells went silent. The lights snapped off. A few groans and then it felt like a blanket of cold space crossed their bodies.

Rumors circulated that Shakib's brothers would be executed a couple of days before him. He did not hear where in the prison they were, how they were taking the news of their execution, whether they would be given time to see or comfort each other.

Shakib had played four years of soccer in high school so he was in better shape than many of the other prisoners, but after a month in a mostly dark room, his eyes were slower to focus, his body worn down by sleeplessness and malnutrition. His uncle,

who had some influence in the government, was trying to get
him and his brothers released from the prison but his efforts were
too slow to pay off.

Shakib was in his cell when he heard his brother one morning. "Allah-u-akbar," Ahmad shouted and his friends followed
him in chorus.

Asghar explained what was happening. "They tie them to
wooden beams at the middle of the prison courtyard and the
firing squad are brought in." Voices of resistance echoed through
the Policharkhi Prison and fell upon Shakib like razors. Abruptly,
a sound ended all these shouts: the command to aim and fire.
Shakib closed his eyes, imagining the slumping of his brother's
exhausted body. From that body, he imagined blood taken to the
air like red leaves blown on the winter wind, the crumpled body
righting itself by grasping the ladder-like shafts of sunlight.

On the night of his first brother's execution, Shakib's uncle
was granted permission to visit. He leaned his grizzled head between the bars, and whispered, "The guard will unlock this gate
for only five minutes. You will need to wait for him, watch him,
and leave as quickly as you can."

Shakib, still on his haunches in the shadows of the cell, rubbing his legs, asked, "How will the guard not be killed?"

"I've paid him. He, too, will escape."

Then his uncle was gone.

That night, after the lights switched off for a second time, the
two prisoners saw the guard; he was wearing a blanket around his
shoulders, and approached the cell looking in both directions.
They could hear the unlatching of the lock.

"Come, Asghar." Shakib had to lift him to his feet and held
him by his arm. "Remember what you told me earlier. That you
were going to eat your mother's delicious bolanis. You promised
me that we'd stay in touch, that you'd be my brother now. I'm

counting on you arriving at your mother's house. You need to walk. Your legs will get stronger as soon as you taste freedom."

The two of them hobbled down the prison hall, holding onto the cell bars. They had probably isolated Shakib's eldest brother for assassination the next morning. Neither Shakib nor Asghar believed they would escape. They waited on a guard or a locked door to stop them, and for the first time Shakib shared the terror Asghar had told him he lived with, woke up with and slept with, so heavy it was like a stone on his chest.

Outside, a mist crept over the wire fencing of the jail. The two brothers hugged and promised they would meet again. They separated in the cold and climbed the clanking fence. Shakib came upon a car on the bank of the road. He tapped the window with his bruised knuckles. A young man in a Russian uniform was sleeping, a bottle of vodka between his thighs. Again, Shakib knocked on the glass. "Comrade," he said in Russian, "You'll get shot sitting in your car in the middle of the street."

The Russian slurred, "What do you care? It's you people who are killing us."

Shakib used his Russian, keeping his rage from his voice. "Not all of us. One day I will visit your homeland. My father studied in Moscow. Now, I need to get to the bus stand. And you need to sober up. Open the door and take me."

"I'm too drunk to drive," the young soldier said.

"Move over and I'll take you there," Shakib said. "I'll leave the car in a place that'll be safer for you to sleep."

At the wheel of the car, Shakib looked at the wreckage of Kabul, knowing its few buildings were crawling with mujahedeen ready to shoot any remaining soviets, especially one drunk and alone. He thought, while the soldier slumped against the glass, that in the morning a bullet would have passed through his pickled brain. He parked at the side of a building with anti-

Russian graffiti, said so long to his "comrade," and slipped across the street to the bus stand.

Walking through the now empty bus terminal, he was overcome with fear and anguish. There was nobody and no vehicles. He wandered in the cold, his body aching. He saw nothing glorious about his brothers' death. In fact, after imagining him free of his body and his pain, he felt his own body like a battered suitcase he had to carry. He thought he was the loneliest and most frightened man ever. After a while, he saw a car's headlights from the distance. It was a lorry. The driver stopped and glanced at him.

*Az koja meyaye o bacha? Da e nawqat shaw da sarak tanha che mikoni?* Asked the driver, who was Afghan but wearing a Russian military uniform. "Where are you coming from? What are you doing on the street at this late night alone?"

"How far are you going? I'm trying to get to Herat."

"I cannot take you in the front. If you want, you can climb up on the back of the lorry. "

"Thank you, sir," Shakib said and climbed up the side. He slid under the tarp to try and get some warmth. The lorry started moving. On the unpaved roads, the lorry shook like an old Soviet washing machine. Suddenly, something fell on his feet; something heavy and soft. He turned on his flashlight and saw something wrapped in burlap. When he pulled the cloth away he saw his brother's face, blue and swollen, the eyes still open and looking upward, as though for mercy. He could barely keep himself from shouting. For a minute or two, he gazed at Ahmad's bruised face, his oldest brother and caretaker after his father's death. *Brother.*

He could not do anything, couldn't cry or shout, but only held his brother's dead body in his aching arms. On that night, the lorry was carrying Ahmad and other corpses somewhere to bury. The car stopped and the driver shouted for him to step down. He left his brother's body to the further anonymous brutalities of the war.

Somehow he walked. Herat looked defeated and empty, and the voice of the man with the nail clippers displayed on his blanket on the ground was Shakib's return to the living, to the desperate transactions of poor men that defined life at that time.

Shakib hitched another ride to the village where his mother and sisters were hiding. Dihzaq in Gozara district was around twenty kilometers from the city. It had been almost ten years since Shakib last traveled there. On the way, the trees, barren, like witches' brooms, shook, as if in laughter at his doom. It took almost an hour for him to get to the house. He hesitated to knock on the door. *What will I tell my mother and sisters about my brothers?* As he knocked on the door, the heaviness of that question rose to his throat until he couldn't breathe. The door opened. He looked up and saw his mother's face standing at the doorstep, stunned to see him, her eyes awash in tears. Everything muted as he hugged his mother, his bag falling from his shoulder and landing with a thud behind him. As she clung to him, he felt a sharp pain shoot through his chest and fell to the ground.

"Brother," he said.

Shakib's mother told Asghar this a year later when he tracked down his house outside of Herat. The Russians were gone, but his family was still in hiding. She made tea, at first composed, and offered Asghar homemade cookies. "I don't know why Shakib said 'brother' before he died," she wondered aloud. Asghar didn't tell her what they'd heard in the prison nor mention their own pact. Then, sitting on the mattress, she said simply, "Shakib died from a heart attack in Ibn Sina Hospital in Mashhad, Iran. It was just a week before his twenty-fifth birthday." She wiped his picture lovingly; then proceeded to wipe the pictures of all the brothers. But there were no tears left in her, just a deep, confounded expression, as though she were turning the muteness of the universe back on itself.

It didn't surprise Asghar. A brother knows when his brother's bravery hides defeat; he'd seen it even in their dark cell. Asghar only looked at Shakib's mother, hoping she'd recognize him, and all those returning from the prisons, as her sons.

# THE SEA FLOOR

## KHALID AHMAD ATIF

✤ ✤ ✤ ✤ ✤ ✤ ✤ ✤ ✤ ✤ ✤ ✤ ✤

It was dawn, 2004, the stars still shining over Shoraback district's American base on the front line of the Kandahar/Pakistan border. The Marines were monitoring the Afghan National Army, which was responsible for keeping illegal activities from the district. Shoraback was well-known as Islami Tahreek's territory, an ants' nest for producing Taliban insurgents. They would sneak in from Pakistan to Afghanistan and swarm.

That morning I drew up my pillow and lay down to sleep. The majority of soldiers were already sleeping when my heart started ticking. A loud siren, an emergency announcement, instructions to take cover, to stay away from the windows. On and on it went, a repeated recording, threatening in its mechanical way. We took our weapons, afraid and perspiring from a probable attack. Everyone scattered. After a few minutes, we heard "All Clear." Later we found out that someone had mistakenly pressed the siren. There was no attack. But what concerned me were the few seconds in which I realized that I did not know what to do, which direction to run, whether to crouch, where the attack might be coming from.

Around noon we loaded two H2 Hummers with some IT items, personal belongings, and portable tents. Lieutenant-Colonel Michael Stroup was the lead in-charge for this delivery and Major Adam was second in-charge. I had recently joined as an interpreter with the U.S. Armed Forces and this was my first mission from Kandahar to Shoraback. After a few days on the site visits, I consistently asked Colonel Stroup to let me be part of the team. He allowed me to work with them; my English was good and he needed it. After getting clearance from Kandahar Airfield, we were told to take the reg (desert) route instead of the main road. With thirteen marines we left the compound, singing the old Marine songs. I did not completely understand the meaning of the songs but hummed along with them anyway. It was a long, boring trip. Mr. Smith was in the hot shield spot, manning the machine gun on top of our Hummer. It was unusual for this type of vehicle to be outfitted this way; normally hot shields were reserved for military tanks with MK-19 machine guns. First-Lieutenant Brian forgot to wear his underwear during the emergency "duck and cover" early that morning. We were teasing him, asking, "What will happen if you're stuck, pants down, in the middle of the battlefield?"

"That'll be my gift to the enemy," he said.

We had enough water, Meals Ready to Eat, medical supplies, and a K-9 occupying the seat for sniffing suspicious chemicals. During the trip we were on alert because anything can happen while driving the mountainous areas, in the crags of those giant rocks. Just then, Colonel Stroup got a call. A small team was chosen to visit a village en route, one that stood at the top of a mountain, one so steep they called it a cliff-side dwelling. A humanitarian operation, they called it, after an earlier botched operation in which civilians were wounded. Days earlier, they had seen men carrying RPGs to the top of the mountain.

"We have to do this quickly," Colonel Stroup announced. "We're gonna have to pull this vehicle up by hand." He called it, "Mission to Mars." That's how it appeared to us all, even the Afghans.

*     *     *

The *darya*, a circular Afghan traditional instrument made from the skin of cows, produced a hollow rhythm. The relatives were singing songs on the old bus making its way from Quetta, Pakistan. One of the old women had pulled her chador back, her mouth full of gapped teeth, and her voice booming, "Ah, Naeem! Naeem! My son, we are finally able to bring your spouse to our home!" They had married just two days before, but because of Naeem's job, selling shoes that came from Pakistan, the wedding had been a long promise, one that Naeem, in his loneliness, sometimes doubted. The roads from Pakistan had been blockaded while Americans cleared the insurgents from the passes. Now at last, they could travel.

Naeem smiled timidly. His mother was getting a little carried away. Her face, normally furrowed and full of worry, seemed almost girlish to him as she conducted the bus in their rousing songs. Naeem's wife was sitting at the back of the bus with the other women, but his mother had come to the front and was now in full command. Naeem's closest friend, who shared his quietness and always seemed worried about finding work and a wife, was congratulating him, though with a sadness in his voice. Naeem constantly thought of how he could one day put Sajad, his friend, to work, but having just married, he couldn't ask anything of his boss.

As the sun began to cut between the sharp angles of the mountains, Naeem's mother told him that they should continue driving and arrive in Kandahar as soon as possible so they could settle in their family home and make his new wife comfortable. Naeem replied, "Don't you think we should wait until tomorrow? It's getting dark and there's no guarantee that the militia have been entirely removed." But his mother insisted. She could make her voice sound like a mewling cat and not stop until he complied with her.

Naeem told the driver, "I know a shortcut." The driver, blowing smoke out the cracked window of the bus, said, "Straight to your bride!" His Pashto was gruff, and he took great humor in his own jokes. The road began to flatten out and was covered with sand. "Aaow waie!" The driver said, the vehicle slipping on the surface. It was rapidly growing dark, and easy for even an accustomed driver to lose his way. After a while, the music stopped. Most of the children were very hungry. The ladies were tired, too, and began resting their heads on each other's shoulders. The men began to settle in. The driver whispered to Naeem that he was using the stars as his compass.

Five armed people appeared from behind the high, rugged crags in front of the bus, almost twenty meters away, pointing their guns and shouting.

"Come down! Hold it there!" One of the men, covering his face with a handkerchief, gestured with an AK-47 at the driver. Naeem told the driver to keep going, run them over if he had to. Then he changed his mind. His family members were with him and he did not want to jeopardize their lives. Or he did not want to jeopardize his own life. In either case, he finally told the driver to stop. In moments like this, one can never know what the motivations are; the driver had followed the stars and, in that moment, the nervous clarity in Naeem's voice.

Naeem thought that these armed people would be insurgents or thieves; the difference could be critical. A long silence spread over the bus as the men outside approached and looked in through the windows, rubbing them with cloth, as though they'd uncovered something they'd never seen before, something fallen from space. They just moved around the bus, and the women covered their faces, the driver turned the lights off, but the men used flashlights to continue their inspection. They returned to the front of the bus and forced the driver to open the door. One of them told Naeem to come down. He felt Sajad's hand clutch his arm, but stood and walked toward the men. A man outside asked Naeem why men and women were travelling together. Naeem recognized their accent, from Uruzgan province, a people that even Pashtuns feared. He took a deep breath, "It's my wedding party. They are all my family."

The questioner told Naeem to get on his knees. The sand whipped his cheeks in the night air. From behind the cloth, the man asked, "Why are you carrying the darya?" They had seen it with their flashlights on his mother's lap.

How could he tell them they were making music? *Men and women together, making music?*

His mother was impatiently looking outside, but one of the men nearest her window took the butt of his gun and smashed it against the taped glass, cracking it. He then continued to smash out the panes while the women gathered as far as they could, shrinking from his violent thrusts.

Naeem's interrogator asked him to empty his pockets. His keys, some mixed currency from Afghanistan and Pakistan, a picture of his wife in the thin, nearly empty wallet lay on the sand in front of him, almost immediately engulfed by it. The interrogator didn't seem interested in the money, and that worried Naeem even more.

"How old are you?" The man said through the muffling scarf.

"Twenty, sir."

"Why are you marrying so old?" There was a strange softness in the interrogator's voice that might have been the whistling of sand, the elements that would remove the traces of whatever was to come.

"Sir, I am just a shoe salesman. It has been very hard to make the money for the wedding."

From behind Naeem, another man locked his throat in a tight hold, nearly suffocating him. A sudden sharp pain came from his Achilles tendon. Someone was trying to saw his foot off. He heard his wife and mother screaming, and then the sound of two shots, and that whistling of the wind. Laughter came from a man on the bus, and Naeem imagined he could also hear the stunned, blood-soaked silence of everyone aboard, the sound of people wishing they could drown in their own breath. The pain in his foot, as they began to cut through the bone and twist it from his ankle, made him fall face forward on the ground, inhaling the sand. He had never imagined that pain could be as wide as the sky and full of burning holes, like its stars.

One of the men mounted him, wrestling his pants down and forcing himself into him. Sajad, motivated by his own life of humiliations, hollered out, the first to break the silence of the mesmerized passengers. In a moment, Naeem could see his friend being guided from the bus by his ear like an Eid sheep. The man forced Sajad to put his head a few feet from the front tire of the bus, his gun at his temple and his foot on his chest. He hollered to the driver, "Move ahead until I tell you to stop."

The driver, hearing the people on the bus yelling for him not to move, and a man behind him pushing a muzzle into the back of his balding scalp, turned the key in dumbfounded silence. The bus shook into gear, and suddenly they all heard Sajad's voice, weak and tearful, not the voice he would have wished for when he first spoke out against Naeem's humiliation. "Please stop! Please don't drive! If you believe in Allah, please!" Tears ran from his eyes, blurring the already blurry night.

But the bus moved slowly toward him until he felt it pressing against his ear, his hair pinning him down. When the insurgent hollered to stop, the bus still moved forward, crushing his windpipe and half his face. The insurgent called the others to look at the eye that had been disgorged from the socket, and to listen to the gurgling of Sajad's throat. "Again," they shouted, and those still alive on the bus felt it go over the head like a melon in the road.

One by one, the insurgents asked everyone off the bus, demanding complete silence. Naeem's wife and mother were already slumped forward, the blood still pouring from the holes put in the middle of their foreheads. The blood ran around the rusted legs of the bolted seats, and each person added to the bloody footprints through the bus, as though painting its floor. Beneath a rusted seat, the darya was drying in it.

The men and boys went first; there were fifteen of them, the boys stoically holding their father's *laman*, the long fabric of their shirts. Some fathers led their boys, hands on top of their children's heads, as though they had set out to celebrate. One at a time they were led to different points around the bus where small glints of the stars touched the sand. The insurgents didn't waste their bullets. They slit the throats of the father's first, knowing that a father might imagine his son surviving, knowing that it was a father's obligation to show courage.

The boys were then dispensed with, some raped before they were dismembered, arms and legs tied, and stomachs opened with *chakos,* long serrated butcher's knives. Tongues, penises, fingers, ears were brought to different places and planted in the sand, small, tilting pyramids of flesh.

Then, unable to get them to move silently, the women and girls moved off, moaning both in mourning and terror. Naeem's aunt went first. Her name was Shukria. With her sister slumped and bleeding beside her, she walked toward death with a greater willingness than the rest. She had never seen her sister so happy; and it was she who had brought the darya. Fortunately, Shukria had never had children, so there was no one to explain to, no one to impede her walking. When she exited the bus, she thanked Allah that she had no child who would witness the gore or who would survive it and have to carry its memory. A man holding a scarf over his mouth—none of these men tied their scarves around their faces, but held them, as though the wind carried poison on it—took her arm and pushed her in front of the gun's muzzle, digging it into her lower back. He walked her farther than most. When the bodies were discovered, the women were the last to be found, as all of them were taken to more remote areas surrounding the bus. She may have expected to be raped, or worse, gang raped, but her assassin did not touch her. He asked her only to sit facing the mountain. He took out his chako and followed the base of her spine up to her neck. In one quick gesture, he removed the spine from her skin, with her yelling out into the blackness.

The other women and girls were not raped, but similarly filleted like fish, their spines removed, or their intestines lifted from their slick wounds. The youngest girls were killed while their mothers watched, and sometimes, if a mother turned away, the chako was used under her neck to turn it in the direction of the daughter's assault.

The murderers gathered, laughing and leaning on the bus. The last shot was unceremoniously reserved for the driver. His death was like an afterthought, not worthy of the gross abuses they had unleashed on the others.

The stars were moving rapidly. The killers could read the messages of the stars on the sand. They had learned to read the simple world of the wind, the spare trees, the tracks of snakes, light and dark, life and death, though they did not know on which side of these worlds they existed.

\* \* \*

By the time we made it to the village on the cliff, it was already late afternoon, and a silence engulfed us all, a silence that, for this translator, was deeply worrying, for it had no whispers on it, nothing to discern. Colonel Stroup was the first to speak. "Javid, what's your gut telling you?"

"I'm hungry, but my stomach is saying 'no M.R.E. tonight.'"

The men were taking turns getting out of the Hummer and putting stones behind its back tires to keep it from slipping. One man was required to stand in between the banks of headlights, shouting out where to place the stones; the visibility was that low. The ascent left us exhausted. When we finally arrived at the top of the mountain, it looked as though someone had hacked off its peak. The sudden, gray flatness of the area was stunning. We stopped, all five Hummers idling with our lights on. A few mud houses had cooking flames already in the kitchen windows, and the air was frosty; you could feel the ice in it. Some children ran out, barely clothed, wearing the *kamiz*, or long Afghan shirt, but no *partoog*, or traditional pant. The boys ran straight to the Hummers, carrying stones in their hands, and began throwing them at the vehicles, knocking out two lights. "Shut 'em off," Colonel Stroup hollered. Then we heard the stones falling on the hoods, but at least they had stopped aiming for the lights. "Javid, tell them they have to stop."

I was standing with my head emerging from the hot shield, and I reprimanded the boys roughly, "Ma Kawaie!"

One of the boys hollered back, "Konaa ma shlawa!"

"What's he saying?" the Colonel asked.

"Well, it's kinda not welcoming. It means, 'Don't fuck with us.'"

"Don't fuck with us?" The Colonel's indignation hadn't reached its full force. "Don't fuck with us? After we come this far out of our way to provide medicine and food to these people? Tell him to go fuck himself. Get these asshole kids out of here."

I didn't tell the kid to go fuck himself, but the words formulated in my mind, *worza kona warka*. Instead, I just told him to get the elders, *masharan*.

"Masharan ghaie aw ka sapakaie!"

"What's this idiot saying?"

"Well, sir, he wants to know whether we're going to fuck the elders, or what? This kid's not happy with us."

"Well isn't that a shame. I guess Santa gave him shit for Christmas. Warn him that if the elders don't show up, we're coming in."

Another group of younger boys, one with a cracked tooth and another with sores on his face, were fighting over what at first I assumed was a toy, but later realized was a dead pigeon on a piece of kite string. Colonel Stroup, tired of the lack of elders, started hollering. "Get them the hell out of here!"

One of the boys swung the pigeon on the string and let it go, hitting the windshield and scaring First-Lieutenant Brian out of his stupor.

I heard him say, "What the fuck just hit us? A dead pigeon?"

When I told the kids that they were seriously in trouble, the one who'd thrown the bird was standing with a hand on his hip, just smiling. None of them seemed the slightest bit concerned about the armaments on the vehicle. In fact, we worried they would climb onto the vehicle if we allowed them to get any closer.

Just then, an old man ducked out of one of the small door-ways. He wore a large black *paj,* a turban I'd seen worn by many Taliban. He was unstable on his legs, but walked determinedly with his cane. He used the cane to smack the boys, who suddenly seemed compliant and even afraid of him.

"Zai khar hosano!" he shouted.

Stroup asked, "What's he saying?"

"Well, there seems to be a miscommunication." I didn't want to tell Stroup that this elder was telling us to get our stupid asses out of there. I wasn't sure why I hesitated, except in that moment, I thought I could talk the old man down, and that I could keep Stroup from getting impulsive. I also felt embarrassed. I'd never encountered people like this, wild people, who did not at least attempt to extend hospitality.

I told him respectfully that we'd come to deliver medical supplies and food; that there'd been an accident, and that any problems that they'd experienced as a result of fighting could be compensated. I told him that we needed to know what the village's needs were.

The man ground his cane into the earth. I saw his fingers so cold they were split at the knuckles and his face took on the contours of the land, its coarse and pitted stone craters.

The man said to me, "We have no need for anything you've brought us. You have thirty minutes to leave this village or else you will face death like cowards. No one is welcome in this village unless I invite them. You tell your American whore-bosses they will be fucked by our donkeys while we drink tea."

I had never heard an Afghan speak this way, with the confidence of the entire village behind him, and I felt my cheeks blush and my temper flare.

I asked him if all of these kids were from the daughters he fucked.

Oddly, I felt it might be true, that the children's faces had his face in them. And this sickened me, but it was the only imaginable situation, since the village was so remote, it seemed impossible that more than one family would be attracted to live there, so far from water or any provisions.

Stroup, angry with me, called out. "What the hell are you talking about?"

"We're having a nice conversation. He's granting us thirty minutes to get the hell out of here. He refuses to take anything from us." Though I knew I was breaking the code of conduct by not translating exactly, I suddenly didn't trust Stroup or the elder, not if it got really heated or if Stroup decided we were going to insist on going in. I thought I would just let him know that we should probably not engage with him.

"Are you kidding me? This shivering old man wants everyone in his village to go without any food or medicine? He must be crazy. We're going to leave them supplies."

"Sir, if I can suggest, they don't give a shit about the supplies and it could get ugly if we don't honor his request."

Stroup said, "I'm letting you have this one. If these people don't want us in, we're going out."

The vehicle turned around, as slow as a beetle attempting the same maneuver. As we approached the sharp descent, we turned on the bright lights and still could barely identify any valley beneath us. It seemed we could slip off the face of the mountain easily, rolling into its depths as naturally as a large stone. Brian, who worried about the kids throwing more rocks at the Hummer, started honking. The sound of the horn in those mountains echoed back after a long delay. It was mournful, like the sound of human moaning, as it returned to us.

❊ ❊ ❊

Stroup asked me if I had ever seen lunatics like that before.

"Hell no," I answered. But I'd heard of groups of people like this, remote, wanting to remain apart and live without law and, in that way, were without fear. I had grown up in the district, miles away from where our vehicle had just climbed, but word came down that the hills held people, some of whom my parents had warned me were not even converted, and were not discernible to God.

We heard the sound of gravel under the wheels as our Hummer hit flat road. We could see only inches in front of us, and it seemed the sand was creating apparitions, dancing before the windshield and making Brian anxious. "Fucking place," he said, leaning forward at the wheel.

"What did you say?" I asked.

"Nothing," he answered, looking at me angrily. Just then he leapt back and slammed the brakes. We saw the hulk of the bus before us, the shattered windows, but none of the bodies. The empty bus provoked Brian. "This fucking place is full of ghosts."

Stroup called, "Hold your positions!" We had our arms ready. Stroup called, "Lights out," and the few remaining headlights shut off. We could hear the wind and then that terrible moaning.

Brian said, "Someone's injured, Colonel. Should we look and see what's happened?"

Stroup said, "We're not authorized. It could be a plot. We stay down, let them act first, but stay alert and put on your scopes."

With our night vision lenses, we could see a figure squirming in the sand. It appeared to be trying to escape; then it stopped. The moaning became words. "Help me. Help me."

"Talk to him, Javid. See if he's one of yours. But stay low. We've got you covered."

I called out in Pashto, "Sok yai?"

"Naeem," he said. "I speak English. They're gone. Everyone's gone."

I asked in Pashto how many had been there, what had happened. I reported to Stroup that a wedding bus had been attacked and he didn't know if there were other survivors.

I asked Naeem if he spoke Dari, thinking if he did, it would be less likely that insurgents in this area would understand him. I wanted him to tell me whether he was bait.

*Aya kase dega hanoz ham ast?* "Is there still somebody around?"

"Nai, kase naist," he answered in Dari.

"I think he's clean," I told Stroup.

"Send out the canine," Stroup said. "Tell your friend not to be frightened."

The animal leapt out and began sniffing for ammunition and IEDs. It moved around the bus and returned after a short while.

"Area cleared. We're going out. One at a time. Split it up, circle the bus, clean it out, and cover each other's asses."

"Brian, stop holding your dick and get the hell out," Stroup said.

Brian looked terrified. He stepped out, crab-walking and aiming in all directions. "I got a body," he called.

"I got a body here."

"I got another one here."

The calling continued, as I squatted down beside Naeem. He tried scrambling away at first, his mind disordered, panicked, but his eyes wide and begging. "What happened?" I asked, but I could see he was unable to speak and I saw the wound then, with my goggles up above my head, gushing into the sand. And then I saw the foot, still in its shoe, about a meter behind him. "I'm gonna tie this up and stop the bleeding. I need you to remain still. I'm going to tear off a piece of your shirt." I took out my Leatherman and cut the fabric. Just then I heard retching.

"What the hell's going on out there?" I heard Stroup ask Brian.

"I found something, Sir. You need to see this."

In a pile, like sea anemones, the boys' penises were dusted with sand and, in the starlight, bluish. The fingers, a few meters away, rested on each other, like many hands patiently folded. Stroup called me over. "What the hell is this, Javid?"

I stood looking at the bloodless digits. "How the fuck should I know? I got a man with no foot over there." I had no expression in my voice. The entire scene became unreal to me; it was not a military engagement or anything I'd been trained to understand.

Then we heard Naeem say, "They took them to the mountains."

"Who?" I asked.

"The women," he said. "My wife. My sisters."

We fanned out around the place as though it was another planet and we were seeking samples. I imagined the Mars rover, and thought perhaps this was why I felt nothing, because I was merely wires and lenses, something created by the Americans to scope out new worlds. This is what I was thinking as I covered the landscape with my flashlight. And then I saw the first woman, her spine lifted out of her back like the fin of a fish. Then the others, still clothed but for the gleaming of their spines. And Brian retching, crying like a child. Crying in a way that I knew those children we had just seen would never do, would never understand.

Stroup and Brian eventually helped me load Naeem into the Humvee. His eyes were rolled up, still producing tears, and his hands clenched. I tried to talk to him, to comfort him in his language that I took to be Pashto. But he winced at the sound of it and again said he spoke English.

"We're going to get you help," I told him. What from, I was still unsure.

✳ ✳ ✳

Ten months later I officially resigned from the U.S. Armed Forces. Stroup was sorry to see me go. Brian was discharged; it wasn't clear if he'd left for psychological reasons. He may have claimed something else, but even returning that night with Naeem, his behavior seemed erratic and fidgety, and I didn't blame him for fearing every gap in the mountains, every loose grain of sand sweeping over the vehicle.

During the months I considered leaving, I remained at the sea floor, continuing to visualize those body parts in the sand, that bus we had come upon that looked as rusted as a drowned ship. Without concentration, I could do nothing, not even close my eyes and rest.

I'd heard that Naeem was transferred to a good American military hospital at Bagram. The day before I would have to turn in my uniform, I flew from Kandahar to see him. It was, they told me, a good day for Naeem. They had fit him with a prosthetic foot. He was walking on it with crutches when I entered the physical therapy wing of the hospital. I introduced myself as the person who'd found him. He sat down beside me. "I know who you are," he said.

He pulled a box from beneath the bunk and lifted the paper off a new pair of shoes. He seemed uninterested in speaking with me and instead worked the shoe onto the prosthetic.

I joked, "It won't pinch if the shoe doesn't fit perfectly."

"You're right," he said. He smiled for the first time.

I sat for a few minutes watching him, then asked what I'd wanted to ask from the moment we discovered him. "Who did this to you? Were they Taliban, Hakani, insurgents?" I don't know why it would have mattered then; I was done with the battlefield.

He stiffened. "They weren't people; they had no identities. They weren't animals. They were like shadows that pass across the mountains."

# THE WALK

## HOSHANG SULAIMANZADA

✤ ✤ ✤ ✤ ✤ ✤ ✤ ✤ ✤ ✤ ✤ ✤ ✤

Oftentimes the bus on which my adopted brother works picks me up and takes me home. Now, I keep looking back, hoping to see it. We live in another corner of the city in a small, poorly located house: my mother, two little brothers and Little Nabi. Having lost his mother and father very young, our family had taken him in during better times, before my father moved to Russia.

I still have to walk ten kilometers to get home. While walking, I think, why didn't my father send us money for this month? Has something bad happened to him? Will he send us money anymore? His friend who normally retrieved the hawala money just said, "Go home. He didn't send it."

I didn't say anything. I couldn't. He didn't let me explain, "Uncle Usman, we don't have any money back home." He turned and left. He was strange this time, distant.

Normally, he would entertain me warmly, calling my name, "Oh, Naweed. Salaam." He would offer tea and fancy cookies and ask me about my mother, brothers and Nabi. Uncle Usman was my father's old friend back in Afghanistan. He would come to our home sometimes, bringing us things we needed for the month while my father was away. We moved to Tajikistan to avoid the war. We live in a poor Afghan community, more like a village, where people build their homes from mud. We had traveled from Kabul, but our new neighborhood, while peaceful, is equally poor.

I keep walking, but cannot figure out how to tell my mom that we will have nothing to live on this month. She's suffered enough, enough to put her in bed. She can no longer go to other Afghans' houses to bring bread or pens, pencils and notebooks. She fell from the second floor while cleaning the windows of a rich family's house and broke her legs.

Little Nabi couldn't bear it and left school to work for money. He is a year younger than me, and my best friend. We tease him by calling him *Little* Nabi; he is physically big and also has big ambitions.

I remember times when we had everything in Afghanistan. My father was a high official in Najib's government, my mother was healthy, our house was beautiful, and my brothers, bigger sister and Little Nabi played together without fear. Then times changed, and my father became jobless. All at once we lost everything.

A honk from a passing car momentarily startles me into the moment, and I realize again I have not done my homework. It is my last year of school. I want to leave it, but my mother won't let me. She always tells me, "After you finish school and college; you will be a big person like your father." I wonder what would have happened if the Taliban hadn't taken power and my father had stayed in his position. We would never have had to immigrate to Tajikistan and he wouldn't have gone to Russia.

I remembered the day when armed people came to our house and took my father away. They released him after a week, having nearly beaten and tortured him to death for having served the government. They called him a communist and infidel. They released him because he promised to provide them guns and ammunition that they believed he had access to.

Two Talibs spied on our house and waited until night, but by that time my father had escaped in a burkha. The Taliban did not talk to women. Even after they became aware that my father had run off, they didn't acknowledge my mother.

By morning, we left Kabul to Badakhshan, leaving everything in our home to be plundered. On the way to Badakhshan, the Taliban fired on us. The driver didn't stop the bus and my only sister, Nilofar, was killed. She sat near my mother in the back seat and two bullets from an AK-47 struck her. At first, we had no idea what happened. Then she fell forward.

After the bus stopped, the Taliban beat the driver to death and unloaded everyone from the bus, but they let us cry in grief over my sister. My mother cursed them, but they ignored her like a dog barking senselessly. They embezzled money, jewelry, anything they could from each bus that came along. We had two people to bury when we arrived in Badakhshan, my sister and the bus driver.

Another person took the steering and drove us to safety. At that time Badakhshan was not under Taliban control, however, the fear of it happening convinced my father to leave Afghanistan altogether.

*Everywhere there is misfortune there is an Afghan who has already dealt with it.* I imagine us populating the world, not with grievance, but with unsustainable, foolish hope.

By the time I am about five kilometers towards home, I am shaking my head, trying to forget the bad memories of that bus journey, and my father's exile. Recently, I heard about a hate group in Russia that seeks out Afghan immigrants to ridicule, torture, and kill, to take their revenge for the lost war and the Russian dead who fought it. While walking, I imagine my father moaning and crying, "Please don't beat me; I didn't kill any Russians. I actually sided with them and suffered for them." I cannot shake the image of his corpse, the foolish young Russians kicking him out of an anger not even their own.

Night comes on. I feel hungry, but I still have to walk two more hours to reach home. My pride does not allow me to ask someone for money, or to ask a bus to stop and take me for free. I know I am nothing, but I don't want to risk hearing other people say it. My mother worries whenever Little Nabi or me are late, and I think we may be late this evening.

I am happy that she has two young guards: Naqib who is nine and Najib who is eleven. They attended school, but always with complaints of not having proper bags, pens, pencils and clothes. When my mother was able to stand, she did everything she could do to provide us the opportunity to study. She was never tired and never complained about difficulties. She would tell us that good days would return.

I am almost home, with nothing good to report. I remember my mother said to bring something to eat. I walk a few more meters when someone pushes me from behind.

"Ah you Little Nabi! Scared me to death!" I shout at him.

"I was just kidding," he says.

"That's OK," and I ask him for money. He gives me his five somonis, that day's earnings. It will buy us bread and a half a kilo of sausages. We go home together. When I open the door I see my two little brothers playing with my mom, for a moment a smile passes my lips, but it doesn't last long as my mother looks at me. She just needs to look in my eyes to know I have bad news. After my smaller brothers and Little Nabi go to bed, she asks me what happened. I tell her everything, about uncle Usman's coldness, even the thoughts I had during the walk. She doesn't say anything and tells me to sleep. That night, my eyes won't close. I sink into my thoughts again. What will happen to us? How will we pay the rent? All that night I try to find a hole of light in the dark, but it seems we will never see better times.

The morning arrives and Little Nabi goes to work. My two younger brothers also leave home for school. I stay home to talk to my mother.

"I will leave school too and find work."

When I tell her this, she begins shouting, raising herself up on her pillows. "No! You will go to school!" I try to convince her, but it is hard.

A few days pass. Nabi goes to work, my smaller brothers leave for school and my mother is left alone in bed. But a week after I visited uncle Usman, he comes to visit us. As always, he brings us something delicious. He brings bad news, too.

Later on, when he leaves my mother, she cries and hugs me tight, telling me, "Your father, your father is dead. It was a car accident. It happened on his way to send us the money."

For a moment, we both sit looking at each other, our unsustainable grief dilating until it is so great as to be felt by Afghans banished to all corners of the world, each trying to fulfill the obligation of families who rely on them.

"My sons," my mother cries out. "All my little orphans."

# THE GRAPE TREE

## HOSHANG SULAIMANZADA

✳ ✳ ✳ ✳ ✳ ✳ ✳ ✳ ✳ ✳ ✳ ✳ ✳

Today is our twentieth anniversary. He left nineteen years ago and never returned. I am at home alone under the old cedar tree over which the grapevines have twisted and mostly died. I have the picture in my hand. It is the only thing I have from him besides the memories of the year he spent with me, and the day we took this photo. I always stare at the tree. It annoys Oman, my only son. He says that I will become a tree from standing so still. He, like his father, became a mujahed, but never left for good. Oman comes home rarely to visit his mother. He tells me, "Don't worry Mom, soon we will be victorious."

I thought we succeeded when the Russians left, but the war still continues and it takes women's husbands and sons. As usual I have to get up and bake some bread for the mujahedeen in the mountains. The neighbors say that they are leading the holy war against the Russian infidels, but I heard the Russians had left our country ten years ago. "My husband forced them out of the country," I once told one of the neighbors. "Your husband was not a mujahed," she said in return, laughing at me. Now she spreads rumors that he joined the Russians, a traitor.

From the window, the tree looks old and tired, its grape leaves dusty. The roots of the tree have lifted from the dry earth. Even its trunk is scarred from gunfire. I look at it in the photo. It looks young and fresh, green as I once was. At this moment Oman comes in. I smile and he smiles with his AK-47 on his shoulder. I always hope to see him without a gun and wish that one day he will come and tell me: "It's over Mom. Over."

Regret. I live between war and peace, the past and a future I have few hopes for. He has grown a long black beard. He wears a pakool hat and his hair reaches his shoulders. Though I try to hold the picture behind me, he sees the photo again in my hand. I have never had a chance to tell him about his father. I couldn't. He hadn't grown up yet. I wanted to; he didn't want to know. He asked; I didn't answer. It was never the right time. I believe he has heard these rumors about his father. He suspects everything. I think, perhaps now is the time. I ask him to go outside with me, to sit on the carpet unrolled beneath the trees on which the grapes once hung heavy, woven around their branches, sweet red lights.

When we are under its shade, he reaches for me, kisses my hand and puts his head on my knee. He eases the photo from my hand.

"Why are you not smiling in the picture Mom?" He asks. Without letting me answer, he requests I tell him the whole story of that day's events. And I remember.

It was early in the morning, nineteen years ago. He surprised me for our first wedding anniversary. He went to dress up and I also went up to my room in search of my bridal gown. I saw myself in the mirror, happy, wearing the same white dress, the veil, and carrying a bouquet of white flowers that he'd cut earlier that morning from around our house. I looked at the mirror. It showed a beautiful married woman with a child in her. She looked like she was going to get married again, but she didn't.

A year before, on our wedding day, no one had a camera to take a photo of us. It was not because cameras had not been invented, but it was deemed satanic to shoot a picture. "Your life will be ruined if you take a photo," a mullah had warned us. I didn't believe it, your father didn't either, but your grandpa insisted we follow the dictate. He would not let Satan ruin his daughter's life. No men were allowed at the ceremony. "How could I let a man who is not our family member take a photo of my daughter?" he argued privately with your father later.

"I am ready," he shouted. I took my eyes from the mirror. I came out of my room. I saw him, a tall man with brown eyes, curly hair and a smile on his face, wearing the same green chapan he wore a year before. He glanced at me. He was so excited. I walked slowly, holding my back straight as I walked down the stairs. He was waiting downstairs with all of his passion. We moved proudly arm in arm. "The cameraman is waiting in the yard," he told me. We left the house. "I can see the man. He is trying to set the camera on the tripod."

"Where do you want to take the photo?" he asked us. Your father looked at me and said: "What do you think, Nilab?"

I looked at the grape tree. It had been designed and decorated for us a year earlier, on the day we were married. Its branches were tied with pink fabric. We were seated under it. From childhood, your grandpa had helped me weave the grape vines through it. I can still feel his hands, how he patted mine while I packed the soil. I watered it every day growing up.

The cameraman positioned the camera and your father told me that we should hurry up. I asked "Why?" He hadn't told me about his plans. He said, "My comrades are coming for me." We stood beside the grape tree, this time without the decorations or my father, only the grapes, delicious, that we fed each other.

Someone knocked at the gate. At that moment, the smile from my face vanished. He insisted that the photographer take the picture. The cameraman put his head under a black cloth and then "one...two...three."

I stood there, trying to take pleasure in the moment, but my thoughts were with his comrades behind the gate, people I had not met before. Your father let go of my hand, telling me he had to hurry. I went after him. He looked at me and promised that he would come back and I believed him.

"So, this picture was taken one year after your marriage, Mom?" Oman asks me. He looks at his father in the photograph more closely, uneasily. "I am hungry," he says.

"I will look for something, my dear son," I say and stand up. I go and look for some eggs in the hens' coop. I find only two. I cook and bring them to him with a piece of bread. Now when he is half hungry and half full, he has to leave. He kisses my hand again and says, "Goodbye."

For another month or two I will not see my Oman. It is just two months, only eight weeks, sixty days, nothing in the life of the grape tree, I cheer myself.

I go to the room and put the photo on the shelf. I sit for a moment and start thinking. I think about war, my husband, Oman. I didn't believe that taking a photo would bring this much misfortune, but beliefs change. If I hadn't taken this photo, the rocket would not have destroyed my family's home. Oman was not born yet, my husband was gone, and I was left to pull whatever I could salvage from the rubble. The men of the village helped me rebuild the house, simpler, smaller. I insisted we build it in the same place so that my husband would not have to travel to another village when he returned. *He must return to a place with memories. Without memories, he could disappear again.*

I hear someone is calling me. "Nilab. Nilab!" It is one of the neighbors. I am late joining our daily gathering when we bake the bread for the fighters. "I am coming," I shout, wiping my eyes.

# THE SINGING WORLD

## MOHAMMAD SHAKER ANWARI

�֍ �֍ ✥ ✥ ✥ ✥ ✥ ✥ ✥ ✥ ✥ ✥ ✥ ✥ ✥

The kingdom fell. My father, who had fought in the king's army, had to return us to our village in Logar for safety. We left so hurriedly; we took nothing from our house in Kabul. For one week we stayed with my uncle and then we found a vacant room in Kolala, a village named after the mud used to make pottery. The villagers gave us some blankets and dishes. One night I was asleep when my mom called, waking me up at 3 am. I urged her, "Mom, let me sleep for five more minutes." She shook me. "Your uncle is ready and you promised me yesterday that you would get up and go." With great effort I washed my face and prepared. My mom put something in her scarf and fastened it to my wrist. She said, "Take your lunch."

I took an axe and said goodbye. I came out from the room and walked across the village to my uncle's house. The village wall surrounded fifty or so houses, and I kept close to it. The wall had one big door for all our comings and goings. I saw a black dog and picked up a brick and threw it. It hit the dog on the side and it shouted, "Oh, oh, someone killed me!" I ran back home and my mom asked me, "Why did you return?" I told her I was scared.

After ten minutes my uncle came with his donkey to our yard and said, "Why didn't you come?" He told my mom that someone had hit a Mullah with a brick while he was peeing next to the wall and the cleric was badly hurt. My uncle took the mullah on his donkey to the mosque where he was to call for morning prayers. My uncle got up on the donkey and said *beya bachem,* "come my son." He brought the donkey next to the stairs so I could get up on the animal's back. I jumped on behind him. The animal groaned.

My uncle prodded the donkey with a "qe qe qe qe," which the donkey understood. It began to walk our three-hour trip. We left the village. I was not able to see anything on the way, not even five meters from us. The path was narrow with trees on both sides of the street, and it was the wind that told us where to go. I had often listened to the wind that played with me, the way the echoes of our old house in Kabul had. The donkey was very smart and knew where she was headed. The donkey at first laughed at me, saying, "I hope you don't throw stones at another mullah today!" It stopped walking and my uncle told me to hold onto his wrists. The donkey walked ahead and smelled the irrigation ditch, but was afraid to cross it. The water was saying to her, "Don't cross me in the dark." She walked backward. My uncle again said "qe qe qe qe." Finally the donkey jumped over the ditch and as a result I lost my small axe on the ground. "Today I want to cut my own wood," the axe said. My uncle picked it up and fastened it under our feet.

After a forty-minute ride, we reached the river. I asked him about his donkey, whether she could jump ten meters, whether she could jump from mountain to mountain. He said she couldn't, she would have to walk in the river. She moved tentatively into the water, then ran, frightened first of its voices that whispered around her hooves, and the sound of her own landing on the wet stones. My shoes were wet from her gallop.

It was early morning and the weather was cold. After we scaled a small plateau, I could see miles and miles of the desert surface. The sand said, "We'll erase your tracks as soon as you make them, but you are welcome here." We were far from the villages and still we rode the donkey to the middle of the desert. The sun grew brighter, but I didn't hear the birds, normally so talkative at that time. My uncle said "ekh" and the donkey stopped. We stepped down and he fastened the donkey's rope on a bush and took some straw from her back and put it on the ground for her breakfast. "Thank you," she said, her mouth full of dry stalks. I took the axe with my sack and started to cut the ends of the bushes, where the seeds, used to burn and ward off the evil eye, had fallen to the ground. These seeds were highly regarded, but for now we were only seeking kindling. It was a challenge for me to make my mom happy with a full bag of bushes. My mom baked the breads and warmed the room with the ends of those bushes, and we just stayed alive.

I saw a boy and a man from our same village arrive. The boy wore a *taqien*, the white, mesh-like hats often worn for religious school and a vest with many pockets. The vest was so worn and dirty it shone like leather. His eyes looked like two pools of bright blue water in stone. The man had brought a caged, gray bird with them and placed it on one of the many stone mounds used to catch hawks in the desert. I asked the boy if they were putting the bird out to capture a hawk, and he said "No. We just let him come out to sing while we collect the bushes." The bird began with a soft twittering, which grew more robust, like the famous singer at the end of the king's reign, Ahmad Zahir, on a stage. For such a small, common bird, its voice was beautiful and commanding, and I understood why this family would not use it only as a trap for a more valuable bird. When the bird stopped singing, I wanted to clap, but by then I had fallen well behind my uncle who worked fast and was close to filling a bag.

In two hours my uncle collected all we needed and he was ready to return home. He talked with the boy and his father, then came to me and said, "You can go home with Khalil when you've finished your collecting." The four of us began to gather and bind the bushes with rope. Then my uncle fastened it on the donkey and left.

Khalil and I went back to cut the bushes. In the desert, I saw rifle pitches all connected to each other over long distances. "It was the Russian military areas where they hid themselves and attacked the villages. Don't get too close to that area. There might be mines," said Khalil. I was scared and took his hand. His hand was rough like the bushes we'd been collecting. The Russian rifle pitches were silent and I knew that many Russians had died there, and had stopped talking altogether.

It was noon when Khalil and I filled the bags and crossed them over our shoulders and walked back to the village. It was my first time having that much weight on my shoulders. Normally, my uncle and I would use my uncle's mule to carry the tinder back, but Khalil and his father did not have an animal, only their bird, who sang for the entire journey back, earning all of our admiration. I was very proud of carrying the weight. We walked for one hour in the desert and reached its boundary. A stream flowing from the Charkh district's mountains surrounded the villages. I was hungry and thirsty. I put the bag next to the stream and pulled the scarf from my wrist and found only bread. Khalil lay down next to the burbling water, rolled over and put his lips to it, just as an animal would. The bird said, "If you liked my singing, you can wet some bread for me," and so I did. I then mixed the water and bread for myself. It was delicious. I had never tasted it that way. The bird said, "Next time, you should bring me some arzan and shah dana seeds. Then I will give you quite a performance."

I took the bag again on my shoulders and walked for two hours with Khalil until we arrived at our village. The only thing tormenting me was my age. I really wanted to grow up quickly and be a source of income to my family. On the other hand, my father, having been so disillusioned after the fall of the king and our exile from Kabul, had nothing to do any longer. He sat sullenly on the dirt outside the village door where people tied their animals. I don't know if those animals spoke to him the way they did to me. But he grew old very quickly, like anything that spends too much time in the sun. It was my uncle who, after my father died, continued to force me to go on those long journeys, until I went willingly on my own. It was then that the world began talking to me without interruption, showing its gentleness and spirit, and even now, I hear it.

# APPLES AND MANGOES
## MOHAMMAD

✳ ✳ ✳ ✳ ✳ ✳ ✳ ✳ ✳ ✳ ✳ ✳ ✳

I was so excited to meet new people, especially girls. Westminster College ranked the best in Islamabad. I had graduated from school in Kabul with very good grades and convinced my father to let me go to a coeducational institution now that we were situated in Pakistan, having escaped the Taliban. When my father was discussing the college with the mullah of our town, I worried that he might not let me study with girls, but to my great luck, he told my father that it was an accomplishment to be selected to go there.

My cousin, Sherzoi, had once fallen in love with a girl who died fleeing Afghanistan on foot. Now Sherzoi is mentally ill. Though I pitied him, I also strangely admired him. I had read the love stories of Layla and Majnun, Shirin and Farhad, and Heer and Ranjha. I also wanted to love someone, to feel the power of love, to experience the feelings of the heart: that energy and that passion. Perhaps even despair.

The first day of college, I was thinking about the many girls who would be in my class. I had overestimated the number in my head; there were only three in a class of forty students. But still I was not worried, because I had a strong belief that at least one of them would fall in love with me. I knew I was capable of being honest, to myself and to her, and this seemed essential to any real relationship.

At break time, I met the daughter of one of my father's business friends. We had once visited them in Mazar e Sharif, and I was very happy to discover that she was in my class, though I had not recognized her as the young girl I had once met. I asked where she was from, and we both pieced our pasts together, recalling the tall trees we hid behind while our fathers talked business. I asked her to move her seat beside mine so we could continue talking.

After a week, having allowed her to establish the rules of our friendship, she felt comfortable enough to tell me about you. She told me that you loved her very much from the time her family had moved to Islamabad, and that you had joined this college because of her. It made me happy to know that she never had any feelings for you; according to her it was useless to be with a Pakistani when her parents intended to return to Afghanistan. Not only that, she claimed she had no romantic feelings for you.

Whenever I would see you, I felt like you were only a shell of a person. You seemed like you had devoted your whole life to search for something that would complete you, bring meaning to your life, blow soul into you. You needed something that could lift you the way a strong wind carries leaves into the air. Despite my fear that you might take her away from me, I still started talking to you and we soon became such close friends that you started telling me about your love for Bilquies.

I felt that to take Bilquies away from you would be the greatest injustice anyone could ever commit. I stopped thinking about her, abandoning all those potential feelings of love that I so desperately wanted to feel. I remained friends with her, and indeed a very close friend, but because I wanted to let her know how much you loved her and that she should feel very lucky to have such a devoted person in her life.

After a long struggle, Bilquies agreed to at least start talking to you. Soon, the three of us went for lunch and hung out together at break time. She repeatedly told me she had no feelings for you, even after I had let you drive her in my car to see the city from Daman-e-Koh, the hill station on the outskirts of the city. But I saw that she was unguarded around you; she laughed more with you than she did me. I couldn't bear to see you rejected by her. I couldn't see you unhappy, even for a moment. I hadn't realized until then that somewhere deep down I had developed a love for you.

After a few weeks of our hanging out, Bilquies confided in me during class, "This boy loves me so much. In a way, I have started developing feelings for him, too." You were sick that day and hadn't come to college. I felt completely empty listening to her words. I felt angry with her; she had been too careful and taken too long to see your qualities and now she wanted to claim you.

Immediately after class, I went to visit you. I brought you apples and mangoes, those fruits that you liked the most. I was sitting on your bed, the words of Bilquies stuck in my head. You were lying down, an arm thrown over your forehead and your legs crossed under the sheet. I moved closer to you and grabbed your hand. You were sick and I wanted to comfort you, but that was a pretense. I feared you being taken away from me and wanted to show you how much I loved you. When you saw me blush, you understood. You let me kiss you on your cheeks without stopping me but also without any reaction.

When Bilquies didn't have any feelings for you, I had this hope that one day you would understand that she would never be yours, and you might forget her. The only one left in your life would be me. But now, things were unsure. I tried to kiss you passionately, to lift you toward me, fearing that you and she would become exclusive, and a world of secrets would screen me out. It was likely that you would completely forget me. I suppose I had become a shell of a person, too.

After a few meetings with Bilquies, you discovered that she was only flirting with you. She had no real love for you; she only wanted to be with you because your attention flattered her. And besides that, your face had character—an unusual handsomeness, soft-featured except for a small scar under your eye that your younger brother had inflicted when you were children playing with a rusted nail.

You slowly started moving away from her. You knew there was no future for you together.

I was happy for both of us. You had dragged yourself out of that period of pain, and I was the only one left to have all of your affection.

You had also come to treat me intimately, at times putting your arm around me, messing my hair, even changing your clothes in front of me. I began to feel shy in your presence, even as you felt more confident in mine. I knew that you must have understood the change in my feelings, but you went on as though we were still just friends. Even the word "friend" became wounding. You used it when we were alone, when we were too busy talking to be bothered to turn on the lights even when we could see the houselights come on across the street.

A new chapter of my life had started: a period in which I read all of your actions closely, imagining that every touch was meaningful. Those were some of the loveliest moments of my life, and some of the saddest. I would always look for an excuse to touch you. If you would get hurt, or if we got drunk, I would hang on you. On your birthday, as I drove you back to your house, I pulled over and stopped the car. I had almost kissed you on your lips when you pushed me away.

"I'm normal. I don't make love with my own sex," you said to me.

I said nothing, just started up the car again, and dropped you off, my vision blurry with tears.

I could see the life I had to pass: marry a girl, have kids, become old and die. No deviations from it. Or I could live in a world of guesswork, where other men might be friendly, but find me abnormal if I let myself feel too much for them.

A vast hesitation had grown between us, or had just grown in me. We would meet each other but only around other people. It was the last days of our college. We never talked about going to the same university, what our plans were. Then the Taliban were ousted. My father told me we were returning to Afghanistan. At my university in Kabul, people frequently talk about Pakistan and how your country was behind the destruction of my own. I am not interested in whom they blame or how they look at things. I am still unsure if it was your cowardice or mine, but I know that love takes courage.

You will never be an enemy. In fact, I sometimes feel more Pakistani than Afghan. I know, too, that I will probably never see you again, and that there would be nothing to say if I did. We might have wives and children, then, proof that we'd both settled, that it had only been an aberration, a brief moment when I was not thinking. That was before I learned what it meant to be practical, to love narrowly, like a stream that separates properties, countries. You can cross it with a walking stick, and cross back easily when you must.

# EXILES IN THE LANDS OF FAITH

## HAMID AZIZI

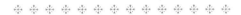

Hussain is a non-practicing Jew with a Muslim father. He's my dorm-mate and—I admit—his features intrigue me. He has yellow hair and blue eyes in a country where this, in itself, is unusual. Our community believes that Mohammad distrusted people with these features, claiming, as they always do, that this is in the Hadith. Where? No one has shown me. His family hailed from a now-defunct Jewish community in Herat. All of them left for Israel by the time the Taliban came to power. They weren't trusted, but tolerated. My own family raised me to believe that the Jews made bread with the blood of Muslim children in order to kill Mohammad. It took me until my teenage years before I began to ask how many times must they make bread to kill Mohammad?

Hussain was raised a Muslim, his father a rigid believer; there must have been intermarriage, another rarity here, between his father and mother. I've never seen Hussain wear traditional Afghan clothes. If I remember correctly, he told me once that he has never tried any on. I don't see any reason why he'd lie. He's comfortable only in jeans and T-shirts, a bit loose, especially his collar, slightly exposing his hairy chest. He believes that girls like men's hairy chests but I doubt it.

"My girlfriends never seemed to find my chest attractive." I say.

"Poor you. Maybe it's your physique, not your hair." He is smoking, which forces me to smoke, since our room is so small that when one does one thing, the other must follow. I get up and open the window.

"What's wrong with my physique?"

"You have a nice one. You just don't know it. Girls like thin men. That's probably how you get them."

Actually, I use the Internet to figure out how to talk with women. Men here, typically, don't. But I allow Hussain to believe that it's my fitness that does it.

Hussain is a womanizer on the campus. Despite the fact that his features would normally cause a father to grip his daughter's arm and steer her off, we have a pretty progressive university, and the girls' fathers are not around. He has one girl he seems to mention more than others: Aisha. She, too, is from Herat, though they never met there. She is soft-spoken, but her laugh is surprisingly loud, and she laughs most in Hussain's company. Unlike other Herati girls, distance from her family seems to have freed her from the usual restraints, and she talks freely, sometimes missing class to do so, with Hussain, whose opinions on everything are recklessly liberal, if not heretical.

Tonight he's talking about his political theory class and picks up his reading from *The Future of an Illusion*. "Listen to this Mustafa," he says, exhaling and putting his cigarette out on a plate of French fries. "'It would indeed be very nice if there were a God who was both creator of the world and a benevolent providence, if there were a moral world order and a future life. It is very odd that this is all just as we should wish ourselves.'" He puts the book on his lap and says, "You see, Freud understands that we create god in the shape of our desires. My god would be more like pussy."

"I already have that god, and I'm leaving her."

"The Danish woman? You're not," Hussain says.

"I am. We don't really see a future for ourselves."

"No one sees a future for themselves here."

Our room is smaller than other rooms in the building, large enough for a bunk bed, a desk and chair, a mini refrigerator. Neither of us is very tidy, and the laundry sits in a mound at the corner of the room. Only two persons can live here. Maybe we were both destined to be together but what really is destiny? Perhaps, like Freud's thoughts about God, destiny serves the same purpose: it makes us imagine order and reason, two things we have too little of in this country. In the other rooms of the dormitory, usually four persons are packed together in one room.

Our only window in the room, the one I've just opened, sits over the yard where a small flower garden is dying and patchy grass is frequently muddied by a hose the gardener leaves running. We usually sit very close together, elbows touching, on the window ledge and talk. The window glass is usually the cleanest feature of the room. Khala-khadija, our female cleaner, wipes it twice a week with her coarse hands that show years of hard work. Thank god the walls are painted white otherwise our room would be dark as a grave. We don't socialize with the guys in the dorm. They're into practical jokes, but they fear us, or our ideas, I think.

"I'll miss you being sexually content," Hussain says. "Now you'll go back to being your frustrated, sexless self."

"It was more than that. Though sometimes it wasn't."

"Well, I don't see myself getting very far with Aisha. In the end, she's a conservative girl. Maybe I'm attracted to that. But who knows? I'd be perfectly content if she wanted to have sex."

"Maybe you're not trying hard enough."

"Oh, I'm hard," Hussain says. "It still doesn't work."

"Well, if you think you want to marry her, you can have sex. Otherwise, if you don't think her father will consent, you're wasting your time. You may be endangering her as well." The moment I mention her father's consent, I remember that he would likely not get it, being of Jewish heritage, even if he were able to pretend to be a good Muslim. Certainly he knows how to pretend. We all do.

"Once again, you think no one will consent to have their daughter marry me. Because I'm blonde. You know, Mustafa, you're a racist."

"I'm not a racist. Everyone else is. Look, I've been dating a Danish Christian. What do I care?"

"But you're dumping her. And Aisha will dump me."

"I'm not dumping her. There's just no future in it."

"Enough with the future. You're saying there's no present in it."

"OK. Maybe that's what I mean." And then I consider what I actually feel, oddly vacant and unmoved by the ending of this relationship.

Despite the enforced lull in violence over the past years, the present seems to spread out like the city, with no real plan, just a mad rush toward anything new. Perhaps my relationship with Asma was like the city itself, a kind of empty grasping.

It's Friday and these are our worst days. The mullah in the mosque next to us is so stupid and the people are even more stupid, listening to his bullshit and wasting their time—if time matters to them at all. He is saying over the loudspeakers, "These American infidels have invaded our country, they are against our religion and they are here to pervert our children and…"

Hussain stands up and yawns. He sniffs his T-shirt, an indication he'll be seeing Aisha later. He says, "Nobody dares to stand up and tell that idiot that the Americans are the ones who kicked out the Taliban. I don't mean that Americans are honest and they don't have a hidden agenda, but the little space for thinking we have today is because of them. Left to ourselves, we'd be shooting each other and starving." Hussain continues, "My father wanted me to remember the whole Qu'ran and become hafiz and practice prayer, but every time I wanted to become a better Muslim and satisfy my father's desire, I started to question why I was practicing something that has no logic behind it. When I don't believe in God, when I don't believe in evil and good, why the hell should I practice? Besides that, when the Taliban took over, my mother couldn't even hide being Jewish. The community pointed her out, always insisting that her conversion was merely convenient. She had to leave. She had originally converted to Islam so that my father could love her. But in her heart she was always Jewish. Now she wants me to go to Israel and become a Jew. I'd rather be nothing."

"Do you miss her? I mean, can you even have email correspondence with her in Israel, or do they make it impossible?"

"I'm just waiting for them to realize that her emails come from Tel Aviv. They haven't figured it out yet. But she knows the risk. She only writes once a month to say I should come."

Outside we heard the gardener collecting his hose. I turned to dump my ash in the wet mud when I saw a figure, crouched beneath our window and moving rapidly along the wall. It didn't appear to be a student, and with the gardener spraying his hose around absently, I just assumed it was someone trying to take cover from the water. Hussain jumped up, showing me where he'd been splashed down the back of his T-shirt.

"Maybe you should change it, or perhaps you think that's doing laundry."

"I'll change clothes. Tonight is the first time Aisha has agreed to meet me off campus. We're going to Herat Restaurant."

"Typical Heratis. Well, I guess that's as close to sex as you're getting."

Hussain went down the hall to shower and I leaned back in my bunk, books spread around me and my phone ringing with Asma's number flashing. I turned it off with a sense of guilt that I hadn't experienced while breaking up with her.

Late that evening, Hussain woke me. "Mustafa, get up, you lazy ass."

"Why do you have to announce yourself every time you come in?"

"Because I'm drunk! I'm happy. Aisha's probably drunk. The whole world is drunk!"

"So I guess it was a good night for you." I had fallen asleep with the lights on, and a book of Islamic accounting on my lap.

Hussain crowded next to me on the bunk. "Move over." He picked up my book and asked, "You really have to read this crap for business? Why don't you ever study the big ideas? Like why we love, or why so much of life is stupid?"

"I guess I never found stupidity a big idea. So what happened?"

"Well, we ate. And we laughed. A lot. And at one point I asked her, if we were living in a place where there were no rules, would she walk with me in the park across the street and kiss me in the shadows, and she said, yes, in a place with no rules, I'd find some to break."

"Sounds like a match."

It was after eleven o'clock, and when we heard rapid pounding at the door it startled us.

"What the fuck?" Hussain asked, getting up and swaying toward the door.

He hollered out, "Who's there, idiot?" And I could really hear the drunkenness in his voice. Just as he was looking up and down the aisle, he pulled a long, thin piece of paper from the door. It was written in Dari, in careful script, and it said simply, "Down with Israel and its followers." Over the letters, it looked like a child had scrawled a Jewish star in red crayon. Hussain closed the door and leaned against it, showing me the page. His exuberance was gone.

"There's something I didn't tell you," he said. "When we came out of the restaurant, I noticed a group of guys, some who seemed familiar, but none that I knew, and they were just standing across the street watching us. Very obviously watching us. I assumed they were jealous, which they should have been. But what the hell is this? I haven't seen anything like this since my mother's neighbor came to our house with the Taliban. I hate this shit."

I could see he was shaken. I wasn't sure how I was feeling. I had turned my phone off earlier. I think, when it came to Hussain, I was also unresponsive.

"Lock the door," I said.

This time when Hussain sat on my bunk, I thought he wanted me to put my arm around him. There had been something needy in him from the start, a desire to be physically comforted by me, but now I felt very uneasy about his closeness. As had happened with Asma, I noticed that in this moment of Hussain's needing me, I wanted to lock a door within myself, to retreat. And though I was troubled by this instinct, I was also unwilling to look more closely at it.

"Go up to your bunk, Hussain. It was just some idiot. By tomorrow they'll find someone else to call a Jew."

As he climbed up, he said, "No. That was directed to me. You know it, but you don't want to acknowledge how serious this could get. I've seen these hypocrites do this to my mother. I know how this group-think works."

"You had a good time with Aisha. Think of her and get some sleep. No point in worrying." I turned off my reading light, and the room was still except for Hussain's sighs now and then, which eventually became the sound of his troubled sleep.

We were woken the next morning, just after the Azan, by loud knocking at the door. I began to pull my pants on, but Hussain jumped from the bunk and opened the door wide with his underwear and T-shirt on.

Before him, a middle-aged mullah in black garb, along with several young men, stood holding the Qu'ran.

"Why have you not taken ablutions for prayers?" he asked.

"Because I was sleeping," Hussain said.

"And good Muslims sleep during the Azan?"

"I don't know what good Muslims do. Lately they seem more concerned with banging on my door than monitoring their own behavior."

"We have heard that you are a Jew. We want you to take ghosle and come to the mosque."

"I have a test today."

One of the boys behind the mullah, a short, dark kid wearing Afghan clothes and a white prayer cap stepped forward. "You have a test now!" he shouted. "First prayer, then study. When mawlawi sahib comes, you show respect!"

"And who is this little boy?" Hussain asked. "Is that a beard you're growing?"

The mullah again said, "You must come to the mosque and say Kalime."

"I am already a Muslim. I do not need to say Kalime. Now please go. In the afterlife, God will ask me about my sins, not you." Hussain closed the door.

"Thanks for the help, Mustafa. Really appreciate your support," he said.

"What was I supposed to say?"

"You could have started by saying that I'm a Muslim, but no, you just had to sit there drifting off."

"But you're not a Muslim, at least you say you don't believe. I thought you were an atheist. I didn't want to offend you."

"Thanks for not offending me. Or them! Don't you get it? This is a country of fakers. If you don't believe, you keep it to yourself. You tell everyone else that you're unshaken in your faith. That's how you *survive*. Remember survival?"

I took the book off my chest and looked at Hussain forlornly. I thought about this idea, of faking to live, and felt an overwhelming sense of grief and helplessness, also a kind of exhaustion that had immobilized me in the last weeks of my relationship with Asma.


At noon, Hussain was gone. He left to meet Aisha on campus. He had no exams, and if he had, he wouldn't have cared. I found myself outside the neighboring mosque. I took my ablutions and went inside, making sure that the mullah saw me as I rolled out my prayer mat.

The mullah walked beside me and before I'd begun my prayers, he said, "I'm happy to see you here, son. May god bless your parents."

There was softness in him, a welcoming completely at odds with the way he appeared at our door earlier. For a moment, I imagined that my attending the prayers would remove the animosity he seemed to feel for Hussain, that I was in fact faking it for Hussain, for his survival.

After the *jemohat*, the collective prayer, the mullah began to speak. He swayed back and forth in his black robe, and at first began to talk of the insult by the West to Islam. He then began to claim that Jews had infiltrated the local university, and had to be purged. "They would not submit to Islam; in fact, their values are opposite to ours. This morning I met such a youth. We must try to bring him back, or punish him severely. We must be diligent to keep these infidels from gaining power."

Those who were listening around me showed a curious incandescence at his suggestion and seemed like they were poised to find this youth the mullah had mentioned. I felt my knees weaken, and kept myself from making eye contact with the others. I felt now that I had joined a group of persecutors, that I would stand aside and watch Hussain be stoned by a group I had no allegiance to, but who had, in some ways, made it impossible for me to feel any attachment to others. I was frightened; that was the overwhelming feeling. Even before the mullah, upon my leaving, suggested I might find another room away from Hussain's, I had considered it. I felt ashamed for considering it. But in a world of weakness, I also couldn't convince myself that I should exhibit strength. It would not be recognized as such.

I went again to the Khoftan prayer, at around 8 that night. I intentionally did not take my own prayer mat so that I wouldn't have to explain to Hussain that I'd twice been to the mosque that we had both ridiculed for its simplistic followers. I arrived at the dorm, stricken by how I could both keep the secret of having attended, and also finding an excuse for moving out.

Hussain was on my bunk when I opened the door. He was holding an icepack to his eye.

"What happened?" I asked.

"Those guys. The ones who'd seen me with Aisha. They were waiting outside campus and just kept punching me, calling me a Jew, telling me that I had to leave her alone, and that I should leave the country."

"Assholes," I said. But I knew I was being disingenuous. I was relieved that I would not have to explain how dangerous this was becoming: his identity—whether he liked it or not—was now known. He would have to respond, and so I told him that I could help him.

"I know someone who can get you out of here."

"What the hell are you talking about Mustafa? I fucking live here. I'm an Afghan. I go to school. I live with you. I have a girl-friend. Why are you so quick to cave in to their demands? These are just a bunch of goons. I'm not going to make life decisions based upon a black eye."

"Aisha's father will never allow you to marry her. And you're failing school. And these kids will be back. Once they start…"

"Fuck you," Hussain screamed, throwing the icepack at my face and nearly jumping from the bed and pinning me against the wall.

"I have one friend," he said, his voice trembling. "One friend I trusted."

I didn't know what to say. I had never seen his rage, or his fear, or his sense of betrayal.

"The mullah was speaking today. I heard it on the loudspeaker. He was talking about Jews. About you. You have to think clearly. These people don't want you here, and when they make up their mind, they're stronger than one. I'm worried about you."

He released his grip on my neck, which hadn't been strong, but had momentarily struck me as being intimate, the kind of passion Asma would never have brought herself to express, perhaps because she was Danish or Christian, or a woman, I didn't know. Really, I didn't know much of anything, except that I wanted to be away from this stifling dorm room and the empty job and the blank, but potentially violent, future that awaited us all.

"What about you?" Hussain asked. "Don't you harbor the same doubts as I do? Didn't we both agree that the mullah was an idiot just yesterday?"

"I can't be loyal to yesterday. Things are changing, Hussain."

"I see," he said. "So I'm in this alone."

"I told you I know someone."

"From Kabul to Tel Aviv. That's one hell of a journey. Or two hells. Maybe I need to find a place on earth where people use their heads, not their hearts." Hussain climbed up on his bunk. "Of course these peaceful Muslims will come after me. I suppose this is how it feels to be hunted."

I was thinking that, if he stayed, I would have to find another room. He would find this so cowardly. But he might forgive me. It was my own conscience that marked me a coward, and I knew I could not shake off this sense of myself. I also knew I wanted him to go to Pakistan as soon as possible, and so I formulated aloud, while I began to undress.

"My friend can take you easily to Islamabad. From there, you can get a plane to Europe, then on to Israel. Your mother will be so happy, even if you only stay for a while."

"But the visas," Hussain said. "And what do you know about my mother's happiness? She, too, was forced out of here by the Taliban. Do you think we'll share our pain?"

"The friend I have in mind works at the Pakistan Embassy. We can get you a visa in two hours. From then on, it's only transit visas to Tel Aviv. Your mother will help, because she'll under-stand that it's a matter of safety. I frankly don't care if you bond with her or not."

"Well, you seem to have figured this out. And what will be-come of you?"

"Nothing. If I'm lucky, nothing will become of me. I'll be Afghan then," I said, and laughed for the first time at the horror of it.

In the middle of the night, Hussain crawled down from his bunk. His eye had sealed shut and blackened down to his cheek. It was unmistakable, a first marking from the community. He had opened his suitcase and was packing.

"What are you doing," I asked, groggily.

"What I must. I hope you'll think of me, Mustafa, when this place becomes too much for you. It will, you know. One day you'll be forced to think beyond tomorrow. And when you do, I hope you'll think of me."


When I called my friend the next morning to set up a ride and visa for Hussain, I was surprised to find myself crying. There was no sound, just the feeling of tears. I then went to the mosque and told the mullah that I had convinced Hussain to leave. The mul-lah was very kind to me. "God will reward you in the afterlife, my son," he said.

I prayed in earnest that day. I prayed for the afterlives in this life. I prayed that Hussain would find someplace to live.

# HARDBOILED

## ALI SHAH HASANZADA

✳ ✳ ✳ ✳ ✳ ✳ ✳ ✳ ✳ ✳ ✳ ✳ ✳ ✳ ✳

Everyone was rushing to the street. People were closing their shops and some of them didn't even collect their merchandise. The carts in the street that once sold vegetables and fruits were overthrown. All their goods spread on the asphalt but who cared? The cart owners were so afraid that they left everything and ran. I saw a kid playing on the other side of the street in the alley. When he saw people were running, he immediately ran with them; he had no intention of taking his ball. I stopped another store owner; a skinny man swallowed up in a long black robe he wore all the time, and asked him what was going on. He replied, "The mujahedeen are coming and the Taliban are leaving. Everyone should take care of himself and get out." I went back to the bookstore.

I thought of turning the sign around to announce its closure, then decided, with everyone leaving things as they were, I could keep the sign OPEN, and that way, if she came, she would try the door. I took the pitcher to pour some water on the floor and then took the broom to sweep it. I took a handkerchief and started to remove the dust from the books. My shop carried illicit books under the Taliban, mostly detective and Iranian romance novels, also children's books with pictures. Of the detective books, my favorites were the Persian-translated Mickey Spillane novels about Mike Hammer, the angry private eye. They were now on the shelves in Herat after being banned in Iran following the Islamic Revolution. On slow days, I would read these novels, the hopeless, entrusting woman who would visit Hammer, asking him to find her husband's murderer. A few pages later, her shirt was off, and a memorable description of her bra, and his big hands all over her body would keep me enraptured.

My shop was located in one of the newly built markets in the gold bazaar. During those years, gold was the currency that filled in for a lack of banks, and a lack of trust in the few that existed. My shop was well hidden, and my clientele were mostly the gold dealers themselves. It was a three-story circular building, with other shops at the center, unobservable to the public. Under my shop there was a central basement, mostly used by fabric sellers, but also by a group of young boys trying to sell sex to each other.

I started my business with two dollars. I bought just fifty comic books to rent and continued the business until it had flourished into something more like a secret library, a place for a community's prohibited desires. At the time, a group of boys would hang around my shop, flipping the pages, unable to access films of any sort. Under the Taliban, I had a monopoly, but I also felt responsible for those kids. They deserved more; the few afghanis they begged each day could have been used for ice cream or toys, but instead they chose the colorful pictures of superheroes, imagining, I assume, they would one day have magical powers themselves.

After cleaning the shop, I sat on my chair, a stack of large, used cooking-oil containers pressed against the bars of the window. She has probably run off with the rest of them or is trapped in her home, I thought. In reality, I knew I would likely never see her again. Herat would become another city under the mujahedeen and life, as we knew it, would probably not come back.

It was late in the year 2000, and though many of us knew that the rest of the world had moved on from such strict and forbidding conditions, we were used to them. Even the rare sight of a woman on the street would surprise, if not offend, the local Taliban. I heard a woman's footsteps on the floor, her heels moving quickly and distinctly. Sometimes children gave me their sisters' messages indicating the books they wanted to rent. But a woman coming alone was unusual and even daring. I saw a tall girl, dressed in the customary blue chador, entering my shop. She stood before the counter, greeted me and asked me to give her my book inventory. The fact that it was just the two of us, knowing her eyes were on me behind the screen of her burkha, caused my heart to race. I gave the book list to her. As she took out her hand from under the long cloth, I saw its soft whiteness, and the nails painted red. I'd only read of women who painted their nails and lips that color, and felt numbness followed by a warm feeling throughout my body. Although I was a medical student who studied in the morning, we did not have female classmates. Most of the boys did not know how to communicate with women. Her existence—the simple presence of her hand—made me feel strange.

Finally, she said that she had not read many of the books. She spoke in a near whisper and introduced herself as a hairdresser who worked at home. She asked me about the cost of renting books per night. I told her it was two afghanis a day, but she bargained easily for half that. I took 150 afghanis as guarantee and gave her the book she wanted. Her name was Sahar. I wrote her name and her father's name in my ledger, trying to look as official as possible. She left the shop and disappeared. Soon after, some of my neighbors who had seen her enter came and asked about her. I explained she was just a customer, and then I lied, saying she had not spoken a word to me.

Sahar came to my shop periodically. I grew accustomed to her and even began to think of her hands after she'd left the store. If I was reading a Mike Hammer mystery, her hand would suddenly come into my mind, at first turning the pages, then enacting the behaviors of the women in the stories, holding a cigarette, shaking the ice in a glass of whiskey, even strangling her husband in his sleep. Those red nails, capable of anything! In my fantasy, she confesses to having killed her husband because he hasn't been passionate, because he only cared about the news and making money. She implores me to help her cover it up in exchange for whatever comes natural to me. What comes natural to me overcomes her.

Whenever she came and went, her perfume remained for a few minutes, changing the climate of the library from a stuffy desperate place to one in which a woman could lie back on pillows, smoking opium from a hookah. One day Sahar came and after she looked up some books, she lifted her burkha, dropping the excess material over her shoulders. She wore a tight black blouse with a deep neckline. She began casually talking about a wedding in which she participated. She said it was unbelievable. The women who attended the wedding, she said, had worn short skirts and skimpy tops; that it was difficult to distinguish them from Americans and Europeans. They maintained the same fashion and hair we all remembered from the pre-Taliban era. She was talking this way when one of the books fell on the floor. Sahar bent over to pick it up and I accidently saw her cleavage. I imagined Mike Hammer saying something like, "Keep the position, baby." But I remained silent. When she asked me about what time it was, I stammered. Time stood still, or some other silly hardboiled line came to mind. But it was true. After a while she left the shop and I realized, with embarrassment, I had become aroused. What kind of dame could have that effect on a man? She hadn't even asked me to cover up her crimes. Instead, she titillated me with thoughts of those women in skimpy skirts, wearing their hair loose, dancing at a wedding party. I had to go to the bath to take ablutions.

I continued to see Sahar every other day. I began waiting on her. Each time she came, she spoke more comfortably with me. Still in a whisper, but revealing more of her private life. I asked her again about the party, to describe the women there. "Why do you care about the other women?" she asked.

"I don't," I said. But I knew Hammer would have said something better, something like, "You're not the only game in town." Of course, she was.

She said she was married, had been for four years. "On the first night, I figured he was inexperienced," she said. "After the first month, I realized he was just selfish."

"How selfish?" I asked, wanting her to tell me more details about her sex life. I admit, I worried I might not be able to please her. She seemed to know what she wanted. She seemed to want me.

"I've told him how to give me pleasure. I've taken his hand and guided him. I showed him what he needed to do to arouse me. He uses hash, and then, without kissing me, wants to immediately get into sex. I accept it, but I feel so cheated after him. I feel violated."

I didn't know what to say to her, how to comfort her. "Baby, you don't deserve a creep like that," Hammer would have said. "Now you're gonna tell me you want to get rid of him."

"I'm sorry," I said. "No woman should have to endure that."

She looked at me intently and for the first time I noticed that her lips were outlined in pencil, her eyes lined with mascara. "I put this makeup on for you," she said. She looked over her body, even putting her white hand up to her collar, stroking her throat. Then, she cried, as though she were brought to this desperate moment against her will. I sensed it was a performance. I had read Mike Hammer and knew what these women were capable of. Still, she had me.

A week later, one of the boys, Majid, whom I nicknamed "Mad" without him understanding its English meaning, ran into the shop out of breath. He had just earned a few afghanis to deliver a sealed message to me. Mad was one of the kids crazy about comic books, and as soon as he delivered the letter, he began looking through the old battered collection in a stack under the shelf. He had to sit on the floor in front of my desk in order to go through them, and as his attention was so directed, I unsealed the letter and read it without worry of him noticing my expression as I did so.

She had written in an elegant Persian script words that effectively meant she missed talking to me, that things had grown worse at home, that her husband had kept her from going out, that she thought she could love a man passionately if he could only reciprocate that same passion. She had closed her eyes and imagined me with her; it was the only way she could get through her husband's clumsy, groping lovemaking.

I could smell her perfume on the letter. She included a tissue on which she had pressed her painted lips. I brought it briefly to my mouth. I pressed myself against the desk, feeling my arousal at her words. Who was this hungry lady whose passions she had to share with a stranger? But I also knew that we would not be strangers for long, that she was going to tie her fate to mine, make me do things I never imagined. Mine was a good cover: the quiet librarian and diligent medical student. No one would take me for an accomplice.

Mad exclaimed "ahhh!" as he turned the pages of the comic book. My mind began racing. Her husband had kept her from coming out. But I needed to see her, and I couldn't wait for that man to let my bird out of her cage. I said to Mad, "Stand up and talk to me."

He did, reluctantly. These kids were used to being reprimanded, and his expression steeled itself against what he thought would be harsh questioning. Rather, I talked to him gently. "Who gave you this?"

"I don't know," he said. "A young boy in the market. He was looking for your shop but couldn't find it. He seemed like a sara-dar's son. I told him he could pay me two afs and I'd take it." The child of a house guard. Probably illiterate. That was good.

"Do you think you could recognize him again?"

"I know everyone," Mad said.

"Yes, I know. You spend too much time with everyone down in that basement. Watch yourself kid, or you'll get in trouble."

Just then I remembered some fabric that the old man in the shop beside mine had carried downstairs. I told Mad to sit behind the counter and go back to his reading. If anyone came in, he should say I was out for a moment. I offered to let him take one comic book home without payment. I told him to choose whichever one he wanted.

I went down into the basement and I saw the thin black fabric with its ornamental gold filigree. I thought of Sahar and her friends dancing at a wedding party, and I imagined her hips sheathed in the thin gauze, her long legs in high heels she kept hidden from her husband. I picked up a scissor from a flimsy wooden stool and cut a bolt of cloth, not long enough to make a chador, but just enough to create something short, a garment she would wear only for me, for my entertainment. As I folded the material, I noticed a shovel in the corner, and I noticed it with the eyes of someone with greater passion and malice than I'd ever imagined in myself. I saw that shovel with Mike Hammer's eyes: it could easily cut a grave from the hard dirt of the basement floor, and a bolt of muslin could be used to wrap a stiff. It wasn't impossible to get rid of someone unwanted. What was important was that she and I not be seen together.

I returned upstairs, pushing Mad out of my seat, and I began to write. I did not mention her name on the paper. I wrote that I had received her letter and wanted to meet her. I only needed to know when she would be available. I put the pen down. I needed her to be ready for me. I needed her to be wearing that tight blouse again and I wanted her to use the material to make something she could wear.

I put the note in a sealed envelope, stuck it in the fabric, and put the fabric in a black plastic bag. I asked Mad to go bring it to the boy who'd given him the letter earlier. I told him I would kill him if he opened it. Kids were used to those kinds of threats in those days, and they knew they would be killed if they didn't obey their elders. Mad was an orphan. For all intents and purposes, I was a dad to him. No one else was looking out for him. He took the bag and his comic book, and swept out of the store.

While I waited, I imagined what her house might look like, entering the door, knowing that she would have just showered, that her face would be made up, that she would be afraid, and excited about being afraid. I knew I would take my shoes off and carry them with her into her bedroom, so my presence could not be detected. I would lock the door behind me and drag her down wherever we were in the room, and I'd tell her, "Babe, you're the one. You're all woman."

It wasn't until the next day that I received a response from her. Mad carried it in, his hands covered with ice cream. "Don't get that on the envelope," I shouted. "Now get out of here."

There was no one in the shop and the sun was going down. I knew a few gold dealers would come in at the end of their shifts, so I read it quickly, pacing the back of the store. The letter said that she would be alone on Saturday, after 1 pm; her husband had gone away to tend to a sick brother in Kandahar.

I thought about it. It would be a long journey no matter how he travelled. And then I thought I could obtain pharmaceuticals from my medical practice. I had, under a shelf, an outdated book of drugs and their effects. I started thinking we could find out what his brother was sick with, and make him believe that her husband, too, was ill. All the while, she'd be poisoning him slowly. Or we could addict him and she could claim she had seen him using drugs recreationally, that he disappeared for long periods of time. I found a number of barbiturates, most of which had been taken off the market, but that you could still find in pharmacies in Herat. Then I thought I'd let her make the suggestion. He was her problem after all.

On Saturday, I made a pretense to some of the men in the gold market that I had tooth pain. I turned the sign around on my shop and walked, holding my hand over the left side of my face. Not a great disguise, but not one I'd have to shy away from. If asked, I was looking for a dentist's office. As I approached her house, about a half hour walk away, I felt uneasy, suddenly not at all in control of the plans and the unleashed desires and conflict in my mind. I was gripped by a strange sense of urgency mixed with apprehension, wanting to make love to her and to hear her say she wanted to kill him. Though I knew it would be easier if we had a simple affair, without undertaking a murder, I felt that her husband's demise had always been there between us. From the first time she revealed her face to me in the shop, she had begun to kill him in that betrayal.

When I walked to the door, her guard, sitting outside the gate of their large house, asked me if I was the doctor.

I said, "Yes." If she had warned me, I would have carried my medical bag and supplies and avoided that suspicious look on the guard's face.

A young girl opened the door—a neighbor, I found out—and I asked for Sahar. Sahar called out to the girl and told her to go back to her family's house, that the doctor had arrived. The girl ran off, not looking at me. When Sahar came down the stairs, I felt unsteady on my legs. She was wearing a white chador, flowered, the material so thin I could see her figure beneath it. This was customary for the home; an erotic garment women wore for their husbands, not their doctors. As I stood in the hall, she reached over and grabbed a flower from a vase. Purple saffron, local and common, but in her hands it was something exotic and arousing. "I'm glad you came," she said. I took off my shoes and began to follow her up the stairs. When we arrived at the door of her bedroom, she turned to me, dropped the flower, and lifted the chador from her face. Beneath it, she wore a short skirt made from the material I had cut, and a blouse, similar to the one she had on at the shop, but this one so thin, I could see the straps of her bra beneath it.

"I told you I dress this way when I get the chance to do it. I told you about that party. You seemed awfully interested in what we wore and how we danced. I think you need more than one woman to make you happy."

"I need the right woman."

"Well, that's a common story," she said, offering a lemonade made the way Afghans make it, with sliced lemon and too much sugar. She handed me the glass and then touched my face so that I could smell the fruit on her fingers.

We sat on the edge of her bed, and the room was nothing like I imagined it. It was full of her feminine touches, ornate pillows and draperies, decorations unusual during the Taliban era. Even the carpet, though produced locally, was something one would hide from the Taliban simply because it was patterned with flowers, with Leila offering wine to her lover, Majnun. I expected a sad place, with nothing on the walls, no signs of love anywhere. And I wondered if she wasn't a woman with too many passions for the society we lived in. I wondered if we weren't made for each other. I kissed her passionately and threw her down on the bed, grabbing her closely, and sucking her neck, careful not to mark her, but barely able to control myself. And then I felt her body inhaling almost convulsively and felt her tears on my face.

Seeing her cry, my feelings changed. I didn't doubt, watching her wipe her eyes with the sleeve of her blouse, that she was truly unhappy. I believed her husband was the man she told me he was. But I also wanted her to tell me that she wanted him dead. I wasn't going to let her get me to make any suggestions. If she just wanted me to make love to her, I'd do it. But it was murder I knew she wanted, and murder I wanted, but I also wanted her to ask me to do it. I wanted her to beg me.

Maybe it wouldn't matter to Mike Hammer if he was the only man in a woman's life, but it mattered to me. I knew there were hungry women in Herat, with husbands who were passionless, preferring hash or alcohol or boys. But I wanted her to demand that I be the only one to bring her what she wanted, and that meant she had to ask me to help her with the job.

"Why are you crying?" I asked, my hand running up the inside of her thigh.

She leaned back on one of those little cushions of hers, her breasts up and her head thrown back. "I want you, but not this way. I don't want you to spoil me and make it impossible to endure him. If you keep touching me that way, you'll make my life unbearable."

"That's what I want," I said, crawling on top of her and muffling her speech with my mouth. "I want your life to be miserable. I want you to ache for me every day. I want to create a place in you that only I can fill."

"Don't," she said, grabbing me closer to her. "Don't make me beg you to stop."

"You can't beg me to stop, baby. You're a hungry woman, and you need every bit of me."

By now I had her blouse over her head. Her nipples stood out and her breathing was heavy. And then she said what I wanted to hear. "I can't have two men. I can't be free to choose my own desire, just as I wasn't free to choose my husband. I want only you, and that means I've got to do something. I have to get away from him."

"You know there's no getting away," I reminded her. "Your husband owns you. Even your family would demand you return to him."

"But what if I left them all?" she asked, desperate, again crying and this time burying her face in my chest. "You must understand how desperate I am for him to die. I wake up every morning wishing he were dead. Is it terrible of me? Is it unforgivable?"

"You need more than forgiveness. You need to be taken care of, completely. You need to trust your desires."

She reached up and again stroked my beard, the facial hair that allowed me to walk the streets of righteous men, wearing my turban, but keeping my little illicit shop open, and my passions unexpressed. Did either one of us need forgiveness, or could we seal the blame so tightly between ourselves that even God couldn't see the evil between us?

"My husband is very respected among the Taliban," she said. "I didn't tell you this earlier; I was afraid you would have me killed. You dress like one of them; act like them, but you're different. None of those men would listen to a woman the way you have. None of them have anything in their hearts. I know you do. I know you want me as badly as I want you. I also trust that you can tell me what comes next, what I should do to end his life."

At last, the moment I waited for, and I looked at her lips as she bit them, enjoying her weakness and her resolve. "You have no choice," I said. "He's dead, or you belong to him."

"So how do I do it?" she asked. "How do I get rid of him?"

"Your guard knows I'm a doctor. You told him. There are many ways to poison your husband with medicine. But first tell me what's wrong with his brother. Is it something he could contract, or something he believes he can contract?"

She stood up, her top still off, and removed the skirt she was wearing. She stepped out of that sheer ring of fabric, and lay on the bed, now wearing only a tiny pair of lace underwear she could not have purchased in the country.

"My husband's brother has always been sickly. He's weak, a drug addict, but now the doctor isn't sure if he has a bad flu, or if it's the effect of the drugs on him. They're giving him tests, but he's feverish, and lost consciousness a couple of days ago."

"That's perfect. Let your husband think he's caught a fever of unknown origin. I have pills that can weaken him and make him feverish. If he were injected with barbiturates and Lidocaine, it could create sluggishness, arrhythmia…" I was thinking aloud.

I was thinking about getting into the basement and digging out a hole for him. I was thinking of taking Sahar as a gesture of kindness to his poor grieving family. Making his widow my responsibility. I could be called in as the doctor; the guard would vouch for me.

"When will he be back?" I asked.

"I'm not sure," she said. "I expect this week unless his brother's condition worsens."

"We can't be seen together. You understand. When he returns, I'll have had your guard's son bring you some medicines that will make him feel unwell. That's when you can mention that he should go to my clinic. I'll have everything sent over."

Aroused by the plan, she wanted to make love then and there, but I held back. "I want you when you're all mine. Then I promise you'll be more than satisfied."


A message arrived. She had convinced her husband that he might have caught something from his brother. She told him she knew a local doctor who helped her while he was away and provided her with medicine that made her well in a matter of days. The letter was brief. She said, at the end, that I would need to visit him at their home, and to expect he would have company. Things were happening politically with the mujahedeen and there was anxiety in the air. She said I could make a visit on Sunday after the noon prayers and that she would send the guard's son to take me there.

That would look proper, almost as though I'd never been there, or that I had been there, but it had left no impression on me.

I packed my medical bag with heavy barbiturates and Lidocaine. When I arrived at the house, the flowers were gone. She was nowhere to be seen. We went into the living room, a large, spare space with several men gathered, many of them from different regions. Her husband sat at the end of the room, on the rug, cross-legged, and wearing a *chapan*, the long shoulder-coat frequently worn by Afghan leaders. In his hand he had prayer beads made of precious stones. On the wall behind him were three hooks, each with a rubber whip with which all of us in Herat were familiar. There was only a bookshelf against another wall with religious books easy to identify as Pakistani because the pages were yellow. I could see he was a member of the Ministry of Corrections and Virtue, and he was speaking to the assembled guests about a direct message he'd received from Mullah Omar.

I wasn't sure if I had been set up, that maybe my not having made love to her had made Sahar hungry for my punishment. But then her husband looked at me and gestured me to sit. I heard the men, most speaking Arabic, translating from her husband's Pashto. Others appeared to be from Pakistan, and as far off as Chechnya. I sat on the carpet and thought of Sahar in the bed upstairs, lounging on cushions while her husband defended virtue by beating people with those rubber whips.

Her husband announced that at any moment it was clear the mujahedeen would arrive in Herat. Then he looked at me and said, "*Shotor didi nadidi.*" The expression means: "If you see a camel, don't tell anyone you did." The implication was that I would be killed if I conveyed this information. The others in the circle spoke in rapid Arabic, a general, anxious consensus that they would need to prepare their departure. For a month prior, we had heard the American bombing of what I now imagined were the Taliban military resources. It appeared that all of them were worried and sensed the end was coming. At the end of the meeting, the men took their *patu*, or long scarves, out from beneath their legs, shook them out, and threw them over their shoulders. They rose in groups, collected their guns, slipped on their sandals and left.

Her husband called me to him. "You are the doctor?" he asked.

"Yes, I was told there is a patient here."

He looked me over, and then asked, "Do you support the Taliban?"

"Of course," I answered. "Taliban nemayandeye mardoman. Taliban az khodmanan." I wanted to convince him by assuring him the Taliban were representatives of the people. He immediately relaxed and walked with me to the edge of the carpet where he had been sitting. "I am feeling very tired," he said. "I was with my brother who has a very bad fever. Now I think I may have a fever."

I pulled out a thermometer and placed it in his mouth. He didn't have a fever, but I told him he did. I felt his forehead, imagining it cold, how it would feel moving this man's corpse into my basement. "You're very warm," I told him. I then pulled out my stethoscope. He proudly pushed out his chest as I listened to it. His beard was so long I could feel it over my hand. He was healthy as a horse. I'd have to give him a lot of drugs to weaken him.

I pulled out the barbiturates and told him to take two. I said it would make him a bit sleepy, but not for long. I gave him a mismarked bottle of the barbiturates and told him to take them every six hours and then said I would come to see him the following day.

"I'm so tired," he said.

"You'll need to sleep," I told him. I was thinking that by the following day, the injection of Lidocaine would be strong enough to stop his heart, but the barbiturates would have him confused, unable to fight.

"Please check on me," he said. "I have an emergency to prepare for. I can't afford to be sick at this time."

"No," I said. "I'll make sure you're on your feet again."

That afternoon, Sahar came to the shop in her chador. I recognized her walk. She stood at the counter and whispered, "He's sound asleep. I couldn't shake him awake. How much of the drug should he take?"

"Two pills every six hours. He'll be completely dazed and weak. I'll tell him his fever has risen. When I give him the Lidocaine, his heart will most likely stop. I'll make sure the dose is too strong."

Her hands crept out from under the fabric, and brushed my own. Again, my first thoughts of those hands around her husband's neck returned to me. I said to her, "If he doesn't die after the injection, you'll need to strangle him. He won't know what's happening and he'll be too weak to fight."

"But what about the meeting? He's talking crazy. He thinks we'll need to leave if the mujahedeen come. He's making plans, ordering our servants to pack things."

"You mustn't let him take you anywhere."

We were both frightened of the timeline. We had, as he said, seen the camel. Perhaps I should have known this was the time to let go of my fantasy, to say goodbye to Sahar and the evil in my own heart. I had already begun the process of killing her husband. Now I wanted her to show a willingness to do it herself. I wanted her to strangle him. But I also worried she might go with him and take the easy way out.

"You have to be there tomorrow. You have to help me do this."

"I will," she said. "I'll come down when you call for me. Just make sure he's not conscious. If he finds out that you know my name, he'll kill us both." She left the shop and I turned the sign to CLOSED.

Perhaps God intervened after all. Perhaps he would not allow for the kind of passions Sahar and me shared. Mad ran into the shop. He was hyperventilating, clutching my hand. "Kaka, everyone is leaving. What will we do?" The city was suddenly mobilized, a hysteria in the air. One of the neighboring shop owners, running by the open door of my bookshop said, *ghiamat shode!*—"the end is coming."

I felt myself moving in slow motion. I saw the vegetables and fruit strewn out over the asphalt. I walked outside briefly and heard the warning of other shop owners to take care of myself, to get out as soon as possible. I felt Mad's tug at the back of my long shirt. "Please kaka. Don't leave me."

"Go inside," I said.

As the town emptied, I turned and walked into my shop. I turned the sign to OPEN, imagining that somehow she might come. I pulled up the oilcans I used as a chair and sat with a book on my lap, one with a cover of a woman's hand reaching through a veil of smoke. I couldn't concentrate on the story. I waited. I imagined that Sahar would have left her husband, but then, knowing his importance in the organization, imagined that he would not have allowed her to leave his side. Surely, with his associations to Mullah Omar, he would have been moved, even if he were unable to move himself. Sahar would be carried along with him. Nonetheless, I would continue to open the shop. I knew I would do this even when the mujahedeen had moved in. I would do this until the last hopes of seeing her had dissipated.

That night, when the sun was going down, I called out to
Mad, lost in his own world of fantastic powers. I held his hand as
we walked through the empty market, the soul of the city entirely evaporated, and I took him back to my small home. I prepared
simple food that he ate ravenously, still reading the comic book
I'd given him earlier in the week.

# THE PLEASURE OF JUDGMENT
## AZIZULLAH

What do you mean by the Judgment Day that you wrote about in the Qu'ran? Hajar asks God.

God responds, confounded. Explain to *you* what the Judgment Day means?

I wish you would, she says.

Hajar is sitting in her dining room. I want to pray totally naked today, because I am not shy and I'm not ashamed of my body.

She takes off her dress. First Hajar removes her shirt, then her leggings. She walks to the bedroom shaking her naked ass.

Her sister Tahmina shouts at her, Are you crazy? Stupid bitch! She continues berating Hajar. Stupid ass questions! Oh! Your faith is very weak. What happened to you, Hajar?

Hajar, pulling her hair up from the back of her neck and then letting it fall, pretends that she does not hear her sister.

She faces Mecca. After her prayers, she again asks, Can you please tell me what you mean by the Judgment Day?

God says, I will send an F-16 fighter jet to bring you to me, and then I will explain. She finishes praying but remains standing on her prayer rug, the *janamaz.*

A Blackhawk helicopter, all lights, lands on Hajar's roof. Special forces responsible for the devil's security get off and surround the house, using rope ladders to drop to the ground. Evil angels bang at the door. They are not physical bodies, just uniforms with mechanical ears, eyes, and mouths. One of them scans Hajar and locks her into his gaze. The leader of the team, who is the Chief of Intelligence for the Devil, calls by loudspeaker:

Ms. Hajar! Get ready! We are here to take you to God!

I repeat Ms. Hajar! Get ready!

Hajar is confused. God told her that he was going to send an F-16 fighter jet.

A few minutes later, one blue F-16 lands across the street. Special Forces don't allow access to Hajar.

Ms. Hajar, hurry up! We need to take you to God. We are under attack by the Devil's fighter jet!

Hajar understands that the Blackhawk helicopter does not belong to God. The chief of the team calls his colleagues: Team Alpha, move to the south! Team Beta, stand by! Team Charlie, cover team Omega! Team Omega, capture the object. We need her alive. Do not shoot her!

Team Omega consists of five Blackwater-trained security guards. They enter the bedroom. They take Hajar and tie her hands behind her back. They push her naked toward the helicopter.

At that moment, the blue fighter jet opens fire on the helicopter.

The F-16 fighter jet commander reports to God's National Security Advisor: Object Kidnapped by Enemy. O.K.E. he shouts.

God monitors the operation from the War Room. He wants to make sure that his commanders get the situation under control and bring Hajar to her palace. After an hour of fighting, God's team, led by Aesraiel—the angel of death in Islamic theology—kills the Devil's Special Forces.

God's commanders take Hajar to their F-16 and blow up the helicopters. They bring her to God's first military base somewhere between Mars and Earth. After a medical check-up, Hajar is welcomed by God's followers at the military base by Israfil, the angel responsible for judgment. He introduces himself. Now we are in a secure zone, he says. We will take you by Air Force One, God's private plane.

Israfil and Hajar board Air Force One. Hajar slowly steps onto the plane. Before doing so, she turns back and waves to the CNN, BBC, AlJazeera and TOLO TV journalists who have come to the base to cover the proceedings. The plane is very luxurious.

Two beautiful lesbian angels are waiting for Hajar. They are models of the Hur (the virgins awaiting good Muslims in paradise). She has sex with them for what seems an eternity. They kiss each other's lips, caress and finger each other's bodies. Israfil goes to his office inside the plane. He is busy with his duties.

The plane lands at the international airport of paradise. God himself comes to the airport to welcome Hajar. She walks out of the plane, drunk. God changes form to become a woman. Hajar kisses God's lips and then asks God to have sex with her. God takes her hands and walks with Hajar to God's car. The devil's intelligence services report that during Hajar's trip to God's palace, God had sex with her several times, showing her that judgment and paradise are the same thing.

# THE SECOND SISTER
## HELAY RAHIM

✣ ✣ ✣ ✣ ✣ ✣ ✣ ✣ ✣ ✣ ✣ ✣ ✣

"How did you hear about us?" Ma asked at the open door.

"Well our neighbor works in the same NGO with your husband. He praised you and recommended we come see your daughters," said the woman with the crooked teeth. Behind her, other women pressed forward to see into the house.

"Well, I am glad you all came. You're always welcome," Ma said.

"So Sana is the eldest daughter?" asked a woman in a bright orange headscarf, a color unusual to be worn in Kabul.

"Yes, she is. And I had Zuhal two years after Sana." Her mother replied with a smile.

"How old is Sana?" asked another woman with black, cat-eye glasses worn low on her nose, and smoky eye shadow that made her look like a librarian/pornstar.

"She just turned twenty-four last month," Sana's mother replied. "Zuhal's birthday is next month," she said. "My youngest," she added, a fawning in her voice. The woman with the eye shadow simply smiled in reply, pushing her glasses up.

"Ma!" Zuhal called, hoping her mother would stop it already. "She turns twenty-two!" Her mother continued, ignoring her. The woman with the crooked teeth, whose overbite was a bit like her intrusive demeanor, jumped in and said, "Oh? How nice."

Zuhal took her mother's glimpses at her as a sign that she should now pour tea for the guests who were sitting on the toshak across from her. But this time, she ignored her mother.

Her mother finally said, "Zuhal, aren't you going to serve your khalas some tea?" Then she turned to the guests and said, "She is very capable, always active and helpful around the house, but she is just being shy right now, that's all."

"Ma!" she complained again. As she stood up, she took one good look at the three women before she saw Sana standing in the doorway of her room and giving her an approving look. *Go ahead,* she imagined Sana saying. Sana had a way of foisting these occasions onto her, while she kept herself as distant as possible. Zuhal could feel the women's eyes on her as she limped her way to get to the tray where the teapot and the cups were sitting. She already knew that just like all the other *khastgars*—families who came to ask for her hand then later changed their minds because she wasn't good enough for their sons—she wouldn't see or hear from these women again. Once they're gone, they'll just be an inappropriately bright headscarf, a bad set of teeth, and seductive glasses. They'll all become one woman she could jettison from her memory.

All inquiries and the conversation between her mother and the guests died out by the time she reached them with the tray and filled the cups with green tea. She knew that the ladies' discovery of her limp was the reason for the awkward silence. The three women exchanged grasping looks and shifted their postures as though sitting on thorns. She saw their expressions transform into something conspiratorial yet pitiful. Seeing this, Zuhal went back to filling the cups to the brim. She imagined the women spilling them, their old shaky hands unable to manage the fragility of the glass cups. She smiled to herself thinking of the ladies with wet laps, searching out paper napkins.

Sana quickly walked across the room, only a distance of four steps for her long stride. She took the teapot from Zuhal and said, "It's OK. I got it. You take a seat and chat."

Zuhal took two small steps before she dropped her weight to the floor and sat next to her mother, making an effort to avoid the glances of the three women, all the while feeling more self-conscious than ever.

Her mother turned to face her and forced a smile. Zuhal didn't like the look; her mother had aged attempting to protect her. Her mother said, "Zuhal had a birth defect as an infant. The fact that she is alive is a miracle. We stopped having more babies after Zuhal because the doctors said the chances of another baby surviving were very slight and even if the baby did survive, he or she would likely be born with a birth defect." They all gave her mother apologetic looks and mumbled prayers under their collective breath. The woman with the crooked teeth said, "I'm sorry to hear that. It would've been nice if you also had a son."

Her mom reached out to squeeze Zuhal's hand and smiled at Sana who was serving them tea and arranging the dry fruits in front of them. "It's a tragedy that we don't see these minor defects as a gift, something god intended," she said. "I, for one, am happy to have two daughters, and never felt cheated by having girls."

"What is Sana studying?" asked the woman with the bright scarf, now transformed in Zuhal's mind to a kite flying over a traffic circle somewhere far off. They all turned their attention to Sana. Why wouldn't they? She was the definition of perfection. Her mother, not letting her guests forget that Zuhal could also be an option for one of their sons, said, "Sana and Zuhal are both studying law."

"Ma! Just stop it already!" Zuhal's eyes burned as she swallowed her humiliation. *I'd rather be alone,* she thought, *than someone's second best.* She stood up and began leaving, her foot softly dragging on the floor.

She put a headscarf on as she walked out to her backyard. All the hammering and the noise next door distracted her from the words she would have formed in her own defense. She would insist there were no defective births, and she would admonish any woman uttering prayers about her leg. The third floor of her neighbor's house wasn't painted yet. The windows had the wooden frames installed but no glass. The workers regularly watered the concrete. She walked around her small backyard. Her father had trimmed the grass nearly to dirt. He would say, "A man's lawn is like a man's beard. You keep it well clipped, and it distinguishes you." Beside the brick wall separating the two houses, the workmen had left a shovel in her yard. She thought about calling out to them and asking them to remove it. Certainly her father would do so. He hated the neighbors, and hated the way the work was carried out, as though no neighbor had any responsibility to anyone else.

A large brown lizard, its tail removed, crawled in the thin grass, looking for someplace to hide. She practically fell upon the shovel when she saw it, and in a movement that surprised her, lifted it over her head and smashed it onto the ground, hoping to cut the lizard in two. The lizard escaped, but she continued to smash the dirt with the shovel, tears welling up in her eyes.

The coarse laughter of two men, their bodies sticking half out of the window frame, caused her to look up angrily. "Construction work suits you," one of them hollered. She dropped the shovel and automatically reached up to fix her scarf, making sure it covered enough of her hair, as she cursed them under her breath and walked away to sit on the other side of the yard where the men weren't in view.

She heard Sana making her way out the back door. She recognized the confident and bold rhythms of her stride. How she loved the rhythm of that walk. *She is luckier than she'll ever know.* Hearing Sana's footsteps approaching her, she figured the guests had already left.

"Knew this is where you'd be hiding," Sana said as she came into view.

"I'm not hiding."

"No? Could've fooled me," Sana said as she took a seat in the grass next to her. "You know, Ma just worries about you. She knows you deserve a good life and she's trying her best to make sure you have it," Sana spoke quietly.

"It'd be easier if everyone could just accept that I am not normal. Any plans for me shouldn't be *normal*."

"Don't ever say that again!" Sana exclaimed.

"She loves you more than me, but she's so worried about me she can't express it. You're the older sister. They come for you, but you just dart off, and then Mom feels she has to put me on display."

"She wants us both to be married, but I'm not ready Zuhal."

Zuhal closed her eyes for a moment. Sana was incapable of seeing how her choice was putting an undue burden on her. Sana had the confidence and independence that derived from her lack of physical challenges, and she didn't understand how deeply Zuhal desired that independence, but feared it, too.

Sana stood up, shifted her weight from side to side before she stood back and held out a hand for Zuhal, "Pa's home, let's go get dinner ready?"

Zuhal realized her dad had filled her plate with more beans than rice. She now had rice in her beans, instead of it being the other way around. Did he expect her to finish all that?

"Sana, did you add a new ingredient to the beans tonight?" Pa asked.

"No, why?" Sana asked with an ounce of worry in her voice.

"They are delicious!" Ma and Pa exclaimed, as though congratulating each other.

"You should probably teach Zuhal how to cook. I'm loving these beans," Pa said.

"Yeah, I'd like to learn cooking," Zuhal said.

"Cooking? That's the last thing you should be worrying about," Sana replied.

"Why do you say that? Every good wife should know how to cook a delicious meal for her husband. Men like that in women, especially our Afghan men," their mother said.

Sana answered, "Right, because that's my mission in life. To please my husband. No thanks, I'd rather pass."

"I don't mind the idea of marriage, but I don't want to be pawned off. Ma, you really need to stop pressuring these women. I'm not something to be displayed and rejected."

"Both of my daughters should be shown off. I don't know why you both resist."

"Your mother just brought up something I have been trying to talk to you about for a while now," Pa jumped in.

"Oh great! Here we go again!" Sana mumbled as she slowly turned her head to the side and avoided any eye contact that would open the door to the same conversation she hated.

"Sana, I think you should start considering some of the marriage offers you have been receiving from these decent families," Pa said.

"I agree with your father, Sana. I think we have given you enough time to figure out what you want. You're aging. People are starting to talk. Your youth won't last forever," her mother said, getting up to make tea.

"I'm not ready to decide just yet. I don't know what I want. But I know that it's definitely not adding a man to my life."

"What would be so wrong with that?" Zuhal asked. "If he loves you."

"Zuhal, I'm not like you. We are sisters but it doesn't mean that we have to want the same things in life. I don't feel anything towards those men and their nosy mothers. I know for a fact that I can't spend the rest of my life with some random man. I don't want to be part of those families with their fake decency and their manipulations in service of their sons, their little kings." She tore off a piece of naan and nibbled at it.

"You're hurting Father's feelings!" Zuhal said.

Her father said, "Zuhal, I know my daughters. I know better than to listen to them. Sana, its Afghanistan you live in, and it only works out right if you live in it like a real Afghan. I may have given you freedom and your independence but at the end of the day you're still an Afghan. I don't want you to forget that."

"I'm not forgetting it. How could I?" She tossed the piece of naan on her plate. "I just know I'm not ready for it. I want to live for me, not for others or for the society."

"Well, in that case you sure aren't making the right decision." Ma shook her head. "None of us get to live for ourselves, but the world's rules must be bent for Sana."

"Well then let them bend for me. If it's wrong, let me find out for myself."

Her mother sat down after pouring the tea.

"If you're not married, do you know what people will think of us? What they'll say about us? They would think we did a horrible job as parents," her mother said.

"And of course you'd value a stranger's opinion more than your own daughter's will! Funny because it's my life that we're discussing."

Sana, feeling the same frustration she always felt when the conversation got to this point, knew she had better excuse herself. "I have a lot of reading to do for tonight." She got up and headed toward her room and gently closed the door behind her.

They did not stop her.

"I don't know what goes through that girl's mind." Pa said, wiping a tealeaf from his bottom lip.

Zuhal helped taking the plates to the kitchen and cleaning them. She loved helping her mother, even felt responsible for the outburst at the table. She knew part of the reason her mother tried so hard to have her married was because Sana would never concede. And yet it pained Zuhal to see her mother go to such elaborate lengths to talk of her qualities as though she were a broken piece in a shop. She wondered, too, whether Sana was right to walk away from tradition. It would be easy for Zuhal to end up married to someone who would not love her nor find her attractive. *Birth defect*, she thought. The words defined her before she could ever do so herself. She both resented and loved Sana's ability to be who she was without concern.

After the dishes were done, she went to join Sana in her room. Sana, bouncing a volleyball against the wall, sat on her bed. She was the best on her team, her height perfect for the game. At times it seemed she could fly toward the ball; she had a sense of herself as nearly weightless. She could forget her limitations while she played.

"Nice studying," Zuhal said as she entered the room.

"Did Ma send you to check up on me?"

"No. Can't I be here out of my own concern for you?"

Sana moved her unmade blanket from the side of the bed to make space. Zuhal took a seat beside her.

"I don't like them pressuring me into things I don't want." Sana finally said.

"I thought you did want it but just not right now. I don't think you realize how much you have. What I wouldn't give just to feel wanted and appreciated. Why would you simply throw it away for no reason?" Zuhal asked.

"You are appreciated, Zuhal. As for me, I have my reasons, but you know what? We have more important things to be worrying about." Sana jammed the ball beneath the bed and kicked off her running shoes.

"Like?" Zuhal asked.

"Like what you'll be wearing for your birthday!"

"I have a couple of weeks to figure that out."

"Time is racing." Sana said. "That's what Ma is always telling us, right?"

Later, they shut the lights off and Sana whispered. "I have an opportunity," she said. "A sports scholarship. I haven't said anything to anyone about it, but I want you to know how sorry I am that this whole marriage talk has fallen on your shoulders."

"What opportunity? Where to?" Zuhal's voice was anxious.

Sana answered, "I can't give you details right now. But you can see, marriage is out of the question. I'm sorry, but they're going to push it onto you."

Zuhal said, "I don't object to marriage, I just don't like the way Ma is forcing it."

"Well, imagine how I feel. I do object. I just want to wish you a happy birthday in advance. Really, that's all."

"What are you planning, Sana?"

"I promise you I'll let you know when I can. I just want you to be happy, and I don't want you to wait until I'm married even though I'm older than you. Be as picky as you want, but understand that Ma wants the best for you and so do I."


At breakfast, Ma served eggs baked in tomato sauce.

"Sana, don't walk away. Consider your options. Nader's family called again to see if you have made a decision yet, " Ma said.

"You mean your decision? Because I have made my decision and asked you to tell them no."

"Sana, dokhtarem, I know you don't realize this now but we're doing this for your own good. Your father and I both know the family and I'm sure they have raised their son right. You'll be happy with him. Our relatives and neighbors talk. They're asking all sorts of questions. It's not common for a girl your age to be single. Say yes, and it'll open the door for your sister. We will talk more about this over dinner tonight," Ma said.

"Well aren't you just ready to get rid of us. I have a class in half an hour so I better get going." Sana returned to her room, picked up her backpack, gave herself a quick glimpse in the mirror, and called out, "I love you Ma," as she headed out the door.

That was the last time anyone heard from her. Based on what Pa found out from asking around, she was not seen at the university. He was able to get access to one of the girls on the volleyball team. He didn't like her immediately. She leaned against the university wall as though she were talking to another young woman and showed no respect for him. Her tone was curt and her voice rough and unemotional. She was as tall as Sana, but had none of her litheness. Rather, her shoulders were broad, and her arms muscular like one of the bad paintings of bodybuilders on the local gyms that had been cropping up lately. "She went to America on a scholarship. At least that's what she said."

"Well, I know," he answered, trying to keep his expression from registering the shock of the news. "Did she mention the university name to you? Because we've forgotten it, and we need to DHL some of her things."

"She just said she was going to California. I think a U.C. school. When you talk to her, tell her Mayhan says we miss her."


With every relative or family friend Pa would lie about where Sana was. "Oh, she's been busy with studies. We barely see her anymore." "Oh well, she's spending the night at her grandma's." "Sana says 'hi' back; she's at practice or else she would've talked to you herself."

And the lies continued, until the birthday drew closer, when the whole family maintained the façade, but a profound sadness seemed to overcome them all.

Zuhal woke up to the smell of her favorite freshly baked homemade carrot cake. It brought a smile to her face. Despite all the worry, Ma was still trying to make this day special. She could now hear her cousins and aunts in the living room as she stepped out of the shower. Guests started trooping in as she began to cover a blemish with make-up. She knew the story Ma had told everyone explaining Sana's absence. "She is attending a Female Youth Leadership conference at a university in India." By lying this way, they were slowly adapting to Sana's absence.

Zuhal slid into a black dress that Sana had told her she looked beautiful wearing.

"Now there is my daughter!" She could hear Ma coming from behind her, with arms wide open, ready to hug her. "You look so beautiful!" Ma said as she enfolded her arms tightly around her. "Ready to cut the cake?"

"Can't wait," she said with her head down as everyone gathered around and began singing. Before blowing out the candles, she wished for her parents a way to heal, and for Sana to be happy. Though she blew out the candles with gusto, she could not shake a sense of heaviness and loss that she imagined would shape the family from that point forward.

"Someone is at the door!" Zuhal's youngest cousin ran to open it.

*She's here!* Zuhal thought to herself.

A woman stood at the door with a shiny wrapped gift held out before her. It was the woman who'd come a week earlier with the other ladies, the one with the crooked teeth. She entered the room and greeted everyone tentatively. Zuhal said to the woman, "Please sit down and have some cake."

After it was cut and distributed, the plates carried into the kitchen, after pictures were taken, after the laughter and conversations had finished, one by one the guests began to head out. All except for the woman who had been mostly silent, as though she'd been patiently waiting for the party to terminate.

"I hope you enjoyed yourself," Ma said.

"Of course. Your daughter is lovely. I'm just waiting on my son to pick me up."

The doorbell rang, making Zuhal momentarily jump.

"That must be him," the woman said, squirming uncomfortably on the toshak.

"I'll just grab my purse and go out to meet him."

"Was that your son?" Ma asked. "Please tell him to come inside. Tell him to have a piece of cake!" Ma flashed a victorious smile towards Zuhal.

"Are you sure that'd be alright with you?" the woman asked.

"Of course! Of course!" Ma said as she headed towards the door to invite the son in.

Zuhal could hear her mother chattering with the son in the hallway. As they entered the room, Zuhal quickly noticed that the young man had a lazy eye; it was hard to tell whether he was looking at her or not. How predictable. They brought me their damaged son. The one the other women's families have turned away.

She went into the kitchen as her mother called out for her to make tea. Standing on the windowsill, a black cat, its back arched, was licking icing from the stacked plates in the sink. She stood still until the animal looked at her. Its expression was fearless, penetrating, almost like Sana's. She thought of the boy, properly sitting beside his mother. She imagined the cat telling her *Go ahead. Take a risk.*

*So what,* she asked herself, *if our mothers have put two un-matched pieces of silverware together. I don't need to be perfect.* As she sweetened the tea, she told herself, *I'll look at him squarely. I won't keep my eyes down. I'll let him see me as I am.*

# IF I HEARD HER RIGHT

## FAZILHAQ HASHIMI

❖ ❖ ❖ ❖ ❖ ❖ ❖ ❖ ❖ ❖ ❖ ❖ ❖ ❖

"Rahim! Rahim bachem! Where are you?" My mom looks for me, walking from one room to another. I'm sitting with my younger brother in our *mehman khana*, a guest room, with its warm red carpet, its embroidered cushions and low tables and its silver tea sets, reciting today's lesson. I kiss the Holy Qu'ran in respect and put it on a high shelf. Before my mother knocks, I open the door. She is my height, only eighteen years older than me, but still able to smile with all the excitement of a child. "Madar, what are you up to? Your expression seems like you're planning something!" She looks into my eyes and tells me breathlessly, "Bachem, your father is writing a letter to your uncle in Peshawar. Is there anything specific you want from Pakistan? Your father's friend is leaving tomorrow and he'll bring your uncle the letter and some dry fruits as souvenirs."

I always wanted a *rabab*, an Afghan instrument with four strings that looks like a guitar. I can't bring this up to my dad. We're living in a time when conservative Islamic rules are practiced, and playing any musical instrument is forbidden.

I wanted to make the same request last year when our uncle had come to visit; now, the rules have become more extreme, with families being personally threatened, door to door, for breaking edicts that initially were conveyed over loudspeakers. I heard the sound of the rabab at an early age, before the Taliban. I still remember those nights when my father would turn on his radio and listen to the news. He liked it loud. He would sometimes comment, "When it's loud, you hear it with two ears. It stays in your mind for a long time." I would nod.

It was almost the end of the year and Nawroz was very close; families were already preparing their trips to get together and dry the *haft meiwa*, or seven fruits. I remembered an earlier Nawroz, when we could freely listen to the news. While my mother worked to arrange the fruits, my father fell asleep on a floor mattress. I sat impatiently waiting to listen to the song played during the show's break, a song famous for the holiday. I started to sing along with the music, quietly so as not wake my dad. I sang, "Bia ke beraim ba Mazaar Mullah Muhammad Jaan…." The song conjured the tulips of Mazaar. They bloomed in my mind, the colors so rich they rubbed off on my fingers, and there were infinite fields of them. "Let's go to Mazaar O Mullah Muhammad Jaan…"

Some nights, it was just instrumentals played on rabab accompanied by flute and some nights, actual songs. I liked the rhythm and the tone of the songs. Even then, the instrument produced a sense of freedom in me, making me believe that my life was lighter and fuller than it may have been. It erased struggle in my family. I would put away all my daily fights and arguments with my friends. As soon as the song ended, I would excuse myself and leave the room. My mom still picks on me saying that I would sing that Nawroz song even in my dreams.

Now I look at my mother uncertainly as she stands in my doorway. Should I ask for a rabab? She says again, "Rahim bachem, anything specific?" I keep my expression closed. I think to myself that bringing a musical instrument from Pakistan is impossible. Undoubtedly, my uncle would be caught by the Taliban who would destroy it, or, in the worst case, him. I think of our neighbor's wedding night when the Taliban broke the cassette player and the drums into pieces, claiming that it was something prohibited by Islam. I say to her, "If I ask for a rabab, I won't be able to play it." I look kindly at my mom, whose earlier excitement appears to dim before me. "No, I don't want anything."

She leaves without my asking for anything else and I pull the door shut and go back to the room. I haven't heard the sound of that instrument for three years. My father no longer has his radio, having grown tired of hiding it. I lie on the mattress looking straight at the ceiling. I count the long wood beams running horizontally on the walls of the room. I wonder if the wood used to make the rabab is the same as this wood, and imagine the entire room being played, strummed or plucked sensitively, by an old master that outlives the Taliban. I think to myself, *Let it go for now. Make your request some other time when no one will be endangered. If that time ever returns.* But I had already let it go several times before, and if my fury at the Taliban regime came over me at all, it was in those moments of letting it go.

I get up and walk toward my parents' room where my father is stretched out on the floor writing the letter to my uncle. I stand beside him, looking at the way he forms his letters, the beautiful looping handwriting that is music of its own. I have forgotten what I came to tell him, but quietly remind him it's Juma's prayer time. "Don't talk so quietly. You scare me when you enter like that. I'll be ready once I finish this."

It occurs to me that I must also remind my mom that it is our turn to provide dinner to the students and the mullah tonight. I go to the kitchen where the haft meiwa sits mixed in water, the fruits enlarged. "These fruits are so full of blush," I tell her. "It's like you've returned them to life." I turn to her. "Madar, can you ask Dad to write uncle Zia to bring me a rabab?"

She bursts into laughter, and that sly smile she had earlier returns. "Why would I tell him? Don't you think you should ask for what you've always wanted?" For a moment I feel embarrassed. She continues, playing with my shame of asking. "You know, it's going be very challenging for him to carry it all the way here and I don't think your uncle will want to take such risks. Besides that, you know your father likes to keep his letters short." My father calls, "The letter is almost finished, son. I can't add anything unless you tell me now." I realize they've planned this when my father comes to the kitchen door smiling. "Are you going to ask your uncle for anything? If so, do it now."

Two weeks pass after my father has sent the letter. My youngest sister runs toward me and throws herself into my arms, eagerly saying, "Rahim *Lala* (an endearment for an older male), Rahim Lala, Kaka Zia, Kaka Zia is here and he, he brought you a ra-ra-rabab!" I push past her toward my uncle who is in the living room. As soon as I enter, I greet him, preparing myself for the possibility that he did not bring it. He's sitting on the mattress at the back of the room next to my father. I shake hands with him, and lean in to kiss his right hand in respect and he kisses me on my head. I sit next to my mother. I quickly whisper in her ear, "Did he bring me a rabab?" My mom asks me to wait and not to ask about it first thing.

When he finally does get around to it, he makes a great show. "Your Kaka Zia has risked his life to bring this to you." He lifts himself from the floor mattress and struts around the room, his cracked feet leaving dusty footprints on the carpet. He goes to the corner of the room, and from behind a cupboard pulls out the instrument, sheathed in several blankets. Then his stories begin, all believable fabrications, but described with too much pleasure to be true. "On the way, we were stopped by a ruthless gang. I had to tell them these blankets were especially tailored for my nephew's wedding night. Rahim, you still have a few more years before that, so don't get any ideas."

I can only imagine that seeing the instrument would be like a child being reunited with a pet that had died. I stare at it, almost uncomprehendingly, unblinking. I pinch my left hand just to make sure I'm not dreaming. When my uncle Zia extends it to me, I grab it and then touch it very carefully and gently, admiring the craftsmanship, the beauty of its body. I don't let my sister or mother touch it, suddenly afraid anything might break it.

I shout as I step out of the room, "Thank you Uncle! I can play my rabab now! I can play it anytime I want." My mom quickly stops me. "*Chup* (be quiet)! Be quiet so no one can hear you. You can't play it anytime." But as she talks, I am imagining myself sitting cross-legged, just like a professional rabab player, before an audience that has traveled to see me.

The next Friday, I sit in the yard strumming it. My sisters and younger brother are around me. I don't play it very well but I know some of the basics and I find comfort in the dark, resonant sounds of its lower strings. I have my eyes shut and my hands on the rabab; I imagine the instrument training me. I receive applause as soon as I take a break. I start playing the Nawroz song. Every time my finger touches a string of it, my body shivers in excitement. I start to sing the song along with the music.

Someone knocking on the gate interrupts my singing. My mom whispers sternly, "Rahim, stop! The Taliban are here! Go to the room and hide it!"

I hear one of the Talib shouting, "Bring that satanic instrument that produces the sound!" I look at my mom and then slowly turn in fear toward the gate. I stand still, paralyzed. My mom calls me again, "Rahim, go to the living room and hide your rabab under the mattress! Hurry up!" I run to the room. I hold on to my rabab and cry, "I'm not going to give anyone my rabab. It's mine. No one can take it from me."

My mom goes to the gate, "Who is it?" The Talib will not speak to her. "Call your man to come and talk. You're not mahram to me. I'm forbidden to talk to a strange woman."

My mom replies, "My husband is out and I'm home with my children, brother. Is there anything you need?" He calls back angrily, "I heard the puppet music of the devil coming from here. We will break that instrument."

She begs him, "Brother, there must be a misunderstanding. We don't own such an instrument. It must be someone else. It's not us."

My mom's reply makes him angrier, "I won't argue with a woman. I'll report this to the imam. He'll deal with your husband."

My mother returns, standing in the doorway defeated. "Rahim, this is your last day to play it at home. I have taught you never to lie but I just did so because of you and your dangerous love of that instrument. I had to lie today!"

I wasn't sure why she felt so badly about lying to the Taliban. They seemed unworthy of any truth. They seemed only to punish and dispel it.

My father returned from prayers that night and asked me to give him the rabab. I never disobeyed his commands but I was despondent about his request, and as I pulled it from the blankets, I did so as though I were giving up my own child. I handed it to him, crying, and left the room. I knew he would lock it up somewhere. I sensed it was still in the house, though.

The following day, I discovered where he'd put it. I thought: I can wait. But then, it occurred to me that every moment of waiting would fill me with rage and disappointment, and if anything was satanic, it was the feeling of anger that I had for my family and their acceptance of the needlessly cruel times we were living in.

That night, I withdrew it from the basement. There was no electricity in the house, which made navigating the uneven stairs difficult, but it was the shadows cast by moonlight that were most worrying. The dark objects in the room stretched out toward me and for a moment the world of Satan seemed to gather around the rabab, securing it against those who would try and pry the instrument from the devil's hand. But the shape of the rabab was so clear to me, it seemed, if anything, I needed to save it from that cold place.

I tried to play it as quietly as possible but I woke my mom up. I saw her puffy, sleepy eyes. I realized that I'd disturbed her, and also worried her, so I decided not to play it anymore. I asked only that my parents allow me to keep it under blankets in my own room.

A few weeks later, my father and I returned from our farm and I went to the mosque unprepared. I wasn't able to recite verses correctly because I didn't get the chance to review them. The mullah screamed at me, "You waste your precious time playing that stupid instrument and you do not spend a moment reading the words of Allah." I was sitting cross-legged in front of him and holding the Holy Qu'ran in my hands. I wondered, "*Why*

*does he accuse me of playing the rabab when I haven't touched it
for the last two weeks?"* He kept on hectoring me, "I told your
father to keep you from that instrument." He had a stick next
to him. I looked into his furious eyes. *If only I could allow myself
that much fury,* I thought, *I wouldn't need music. Hatred must be
a kind of music, or a distortion that replaces it.* He picked up the
stick and demanded I hold my open palm out for punishment. I
passed the Holy Qu'ran to the student next to me and the mullah
brought the stick down several times, so that I feared I would not
have use of my hands again. I finally put my right hand in my left
armpit just to make the pain go away. As soon as my punishment
finished, I grabbed my Holy Qu'ran and walked toward home
crying spasmodically. Other boys my age made fun of me as I
passed. I would have punched them if I could have closed my
hands into fists.

Back at home, my mom asked me the reason my palms were
blue as plums. She didn't like this habit of our mullah. She told
me to continue my studies with another mullah who taught far
from our house but didn't beat his students. I sat at the table quietly, looking at the welts on my hands. I finally asked my mom
to get the rabab. She said, "It's almost noon and the Taliban are
around. Plus your hands are injured. Let's soak them in cold water." I knew playing was my only way to control my temper and
depression. Again, she refused to get the instrument.

I shouted, "What's the benefit of having a rabab and not being able to play it? I'm going to break it into pieces! I wish uncle
Zia never brought it. It hurts me to look at it. It is better to get
rid of it, and I'll never wish to play it again."

My mother came closer and gently held my hands, weeping
at the sight of them. "Rahim, control your temper. Don't you remember what happened the last time you played it?" I demanded
my younger sister bring it, so that I could smash it.

My mother said, "One day, you're going to put all of our lives in danger with your rabab!" I argued with her. Finally, she said, "Bachem, you can go to your aunt's house in Sar-e-pul and play it with your cousins, Fatah and Javid. That's a more remote area and they both share the same interest as you do."

I went to Sar-e-pul in the same truck we used to transfer our harvested crops. I placed the wrapped rabab in the middle of a wheat sack. My father drove, not speaking to me, but also not angry. He seemed resigned to losing his son to a passion he had never fully understood, but recognized as essential.

I stayed for three months with my aunt, forgetting about the mullah and the harsh punishment I had received. My hands became nimble again, and my playing improved dramatically. Javid played Afghan flute very well. We made good company. He didn't speak a lot, either, which was a relief, as I wanted to hear only the sounds of our instruments. He closed his eyes when he put his lips on the flute and shook his head as he played. We used the backyard to practice and sometimes his parents and siblings came to watch us.

It was one of those weekends that four Taliban entered the house. We were both playing. I heard my aunt calling her husband, "Rasool! Rasool! There are strangers here!" She tried to hold the door shut but they had forced it. Two bullets were fired and my aunt crouched down, her hands over her ears. I heard my younger cousins screaming. They all ran toward their mother. Javid and I looked at each other in shock. One of the Talibs, a lanky man with a copper beard and a short vest filled with gleaming bullets, grabbed Javid's hair and threw him to the ground. He kicked him in the ribs with his muddy shoes. Another one held his right hand high in the air and slapped me on my right cheek. When I fell down, he lifted me from under my arm and walked me to the backyard. There he continued to smack my face until my eyes ran with blood or tears, I did not know. Finally, with a single blow to my ear, he knocked me to the ground where my head hit a stone. The sound of that fall still echoes in my ears. My uncle Rasool begged them to leave us. He fell before their feet, "Mullah Sahib, please. They're just teenagers. They don't know what they've done. Please for Allah's sake leave them. They'll not do this again." Uncle Rasool took off his hat and held it out to them, "For Allah's sake and for the sake of my white beard and age, please leave them. They'll die. Please forgive them."

On their way out, they cracked Javid's flute with their rifle-butts and broke it into pieces. Then they slammed a hole in the body of my rabab. Even then, I tried to crawl toward my rabab. Uncle Rasool put his heavy foot down on my arm. Then he accompanied the men to the door. After the Taliban left, he took his wife to the bedroom. "Thank God, they only fired bullets in the air," he said.

A few days later, my aunt crying, I said goodbye to my cousins and their family and returned to Sheberghan. Javid whispered something to me I could not hear, but I think he meant to say, "you will hear again." I saw tears in his eyes. Undoubtedly he'd already begun missing our time together playing the instruments. I picked up the expensive blankets that once covered the rabab and uncle Rasool hugged me, "Bachem, please forgive me for letting this happen to you. I will miss you both playing together."


It is three years later and the Taliban are no longer in power. My father has aged rapidly and can no longer afford to take me to audiologists in Pakistan. The ringing in my ear continues, sometimes loud enough to make the call for prayer a smudge of sound. When he speaks to me, I ask my father to speak louder so I can hear it in both ears and remember it. I can remember the sound of the rabab, and sometimes, the low, constant vibration in my ear can sound like its strings, but I can't make it sing or sing with it. I hear from uncle Rasool and Javid. Javid has a new flute that he plays, but that, too, is hard to derive pleasure from. There is little I want to hear, in truth. My mother says I have given up my anger and with it everything else. Perhaps she's right. Perhaps, if I've heard her right.